THE BROKEN MARRIAGE
New Hampshire Bears 14

USA Today Bestselling Author

Mary Smith

DEDICATION

Angie!

Thank you for helping me break the writer's block.

You're my hero!

New Hampshire Bears

Coach: Hamilton Baer

Forwards:

56 – Alden Brockman
11 – Ladd Hanes
28 – Edgar Hopp
81 – Zerrick Justice
88 – Finlay Mackey
67 – Gage McLoyd
94 – Blake Naylor
16 – Vance Pemberton
53 – Jarvis Richter
62 – Jackson Plumley
65 – Kyson Wick
86 – Bas Zorn

Defensemen:

8 – Conner Caddell
32 – Walker Lange
2 – Dag Limon
5 – Ivan Rodin
7 – O'Dell Tillman
57 – Shade Wooten*

Goalies:

47 – Liam Green
77 – Jacob Wallace

* - means Captain

CONTENTS

     Epilogue   211

     What's Next   229

     About the Author   230

CHAPTER ONE
Shade

Shade sat on the side of the queen-size bed with his elbows on his knees. His heart hurt badly and was unsure if he could handle anymore. However, here he sat, in miserable pain.

The ticks of his wife's nails clacked on the laptop. Jenessa sat less than three feet from him but might as well be on another continent. They hadn't even acknowledged each other. Then again it was their normal encounter these days. They never talked, short of small greetings or one-word responses to short questions. The last time they tried to have a conversation it ended in a fight.

"You eat?" Jenessa asked. He knew she hadn't looked up from the keyboard.

"No," he simply stated.

"Stuff is in the oven." The click-clack seemed to grow louder as she typed.

He took the hint and left her alone. Sending him away seemed to be her specialty now. As he reached the kitchen, Jenessa's younger sister, Mikayla, sat at the breakfast bar.

"What up, bro?" She grinned.

Shade gave her a small smile. As an only child, he had always wished for a sibling. He wished for a family even more.

"Nes made some chicken thing. It's in the oven." She pointed as if he didn't know where it was located.

"Any good?" He opened the door. Jenessa wasn't the greatest cook. However, she did try her best.

"I didn't try it." She turned up her nose. "I made some mac and cheese."

Shade grinned. "You're going to turn into mac and cheese." The girl ate it all the time.

"I don't see a problem with that transformation."

"What are you doing here?" He didn't attempt the chicken and went to the cupboard and grabbed a can of beef stew.

"Eating mac and cheese." She took a large bite from her spoon.

Shade loved his sister-in-law as if they were blood. She had been living with them for a long time, for Jenessa's sake, but recently moved out.

"How was your day?" Shade dumped the contents of the can into a saucepan.

"Work, good. Homelife, fine. Sex life, well..." She gave him a dramatic wink. Mikayla currently had been dating a teammate of his, Jarvis Richter.

Shaking his head, he had a small grin. Mikayla always kept him on his toes. He remembered Jenessa being the same way. Laughing, joking, full of life. Now, he couldn't think of the last time she laughed, told a joke, or even wanted to do anything other than work.

The partners at the firm begged her to take the full six weeks of her leave after their baby died, but she only took a two week leave. Shade did the same thing, even though he knew it to be unhealthy.

He missed his wife.

"How was your day?" Mikayla questioned as he mindlessly stirred the stew.

"Uneventful." He shrugged.

"Any word on the contract?"

Shaking his head again, he said nothing. In truth, he wondered the same thing. He hadn't heard from his agent or Bears' management, but Twitter was alive with his trade rumors. He tried to talk to Jenessa numerous times regarding his possible trade from the New Hampshire Bears, but she'd just leave the room or give a nonchalant shrug.

"Are you still thinking about leaving?"

Shade diverted his eyes, not answering her question. Mikayla overheard his conversation with the Bears' general manager, Cabel Dirks. He told him leaving New Hampshire might be best for everyone.

"Personally, I would have left her ass three years ago. You're a bigger man than me." Mikayla never kept quiet about the marriage problems going on between her sister and brother-in-law.

Shade had been the one to suggest to Mikayla to move to Manchester to live with them and return to college. He thought it would help Jenessa as well. Maybe it would bring her out of the fog she currently dwelled in. He knew the sisters were close, but even Mikayla's tough girl attitude couldn't help Jenessa.

He transferred the stew to a bowl and sat down at the bar with her. He noticed she was watching a YouTube video of a person knitting. Shade glanced over at her and her dyed black hair which hung halfway down her back and thought how no one would ever think with Mikayla's hard rocker style that she would be a person who loved to knit. Her perfect cat eyes always made him wonder how long it took her to get ready in the morning. She loved black and her torn up jeans with bright tanks and was always loaded with an array of custom jewelry, which she made herself. Although, he noticed she'd been wearing more colors. He figured Jarvis had something to do with it. Shade moved back to his food. They sat quietly and just listened to the soft instructions of the knitting video.

Just as he was about to finish the stew, Jenessa walked

into the kitchen. No one said anything to each other, but everyone gave each other a glance.

"No one wanted *my* food." Jenessa's tone bit into the tension-filled air.

"It looked gross," Mikayla said honestly. "And smelled worse."

Putting his spoon down, Shade rubbed his temples. This was about to be another yelling match between them, and he'd surely gain a headache in the process.

"Whatever." Jenessa grabbed a towel, pulled the glass dish from the oven, and dumped all the contents—including the dish—into the trash. "There. Now no one has to eat it." She threw the dish towel across the room.

"You didn't have to throw it away." Shade almost growled at his wife. He hated wasting one ounce of food.

"Why? Is the poor orphan kid still having food issues because he ate out of dumpsters?"

Mikayla gasped. "Jenessa, what the fuck?"

Shade said nothing as her hurtful words penetrated him. They stared at each other for several seconds before he wiped his mouth with the napkin, slowly stood up and said, "You win." He walked away from the kitchen and went down to the den.

He fell with a thud onto the couch and hated the fact that tears were burning behind his eyes. Her words burnt his soul. She knew how much he detested his past and how embarrassing it had been to him. He never knew his father. Shade always wondered, but the few times he brought it up to his mother she always shrugged. She probably never knew his name or which man it truly was. At the age of eight, his mother had up and left him. He spent days all alone. When the small jar of peanut butter he'd had was gone, he left the rundown apartment and went down the street. There was a pizza parlor on the corner, so he climbed into one of the dumpsters. Shade didn't know how long he had been in the dumpster, but it seemed like it was only a few minutes when the police showed up.

For the next ten years, he bounced from foster home to foster home. By some miracle, because he never knew how, he made it onto the hockey team at a state college in New York as a walk-on. He began to make a name for himself in the college hockey circuit. No one was more shocked than him when he was drafted into the PHL to a team in Maine. His entire life changed in an instant and only got better when Shade met Jenessa.

"Hey." Mikayla's soft voice made him turn, and she slowly approached him. "I want to apologize for her."

He turned away. His jaw fixed as his teeth were grinding. He couldn't fault Mikayla for sticking up for her big sister.

"I told her she was a royal bitch, and she ran off to the bedroom."

He nodded, still not talking.

"I'll leave you be, but if you need anything, please let me know."

Waiting until she had completely left the room a single tear escaped his eye. He sniffed hard and roughly wiped his cheek then he got up and headed to their bedroom. Standing outside their closed door, he wanted to go in. He had the urge to tell her everything weighing heavily on him but decided to go further down the hall to another closed door—the nursery.

Opening the door, it seemed like he was stepping into a tomb. He had come in here a lot the first year after losing baby Clay. The gray walls reminded him of how long it took them to pick out the color. They stood in front of paint samples at Lowe's for almost an hour before Jenessa finally agreed on a color. Shade just stood there, letting her take all the time she needed while rubbing her back. He still remembered how she continually rubbed her swollen belly.

A few of his friends who played on the Bears with him sent Jenessa to the spa with their wives as the guys painted the entire room. He touched the paint, trying to keep the tears away as he remembered how happy he was that day.

He lightly touched the white crib. A small layer of dust built up on the rail reminding him he hadn't cleaned in here for a while. Jenessa wouldn't come in here, but she refused to let him clean it out.

Leaning his elbows on the rails, he saw the silver urn laying inside.

Baby Clay Wooten.

Shade picked it up in his hands, knowing his son's ashes were inside. He remembered holding his son in his arms wanting to die with him or take his place but tried his best to be strong for Jenessa. Her sobbing was something he could never forget.

After the funeral, Jenessa laid in bed for a week. Shade fed her, bathed her, and talked to her. Then one day she just seemed to wake up and went to work and cut him out of her life.

Over three years later, he couldn't remember the last time they kissed, hugged, or even touched. They had sex about a week before she went into labor and nothing since. He tried about a year ago when he made plans for a romantic getaway, but Jenessa pretty much told him to get lost, and he never tried to make plans again.

Setting the small urn back into the crib, he took a deep breath, shut the door, and went back downstairs, never glancing at their bedroom door. He kept an extra pillow and blankets in the den. Grabbing them, he stretched out on the sectional and closed his tired eyes.

After a shower and a fresh change of clothes, he tied his shoes and strolled into the kitchen. Jenessa's light brown hair sat high in a ponytail on her head. She wore a pair of black pants and a pink blouse. She was leaning against the counter sipping her coffee. Jenessa stared at him as he picked up an apple from the fruit bowl.

"Coffee?" Jenessa asked him.

Shade notice her permeated frown. Obviously, she didn't know about his new lifestyle change. He had stopped drinking caffeine months ago. "I'm fine. Thanks." He turned toward the door leading to the garage and said, "Bye," as he walked out to his truck.

On the drive to the arena, Shade's thoughts ran erratically in his head. He fought for every success throughout his life. He hated to fail more than anything. Especially when it came to his marriage, but he truly didn't know how much longer he could try to keep them together. However, he failed to keep his son alive, and now his wife seemed to be slipping through his fingers. He should have been able to protect them both, but he couldn't. His son was dead, and his wife was dead on the inside but still walking around the living. Hell, the first year he did as well, yet figured out a way to live with the grief that killed his soul. It never went away, but the dull ache became somewhat bearable for him to get back on the ice.

Hockey.

Hockey saved his life more than once. As a child, whenever his mother was high or had a *friend* over, Shade would go down to the local ice rink. They had free hours and allowed *some* kids to borrow skates. Those kids were the ones that were too poor to afford their own. After his mother left him, he would still go after school to stay away from the foster homes. Not every foster parent had been horrible, but he had his fair share. He remembered the unnecessary beatings, the hunger pains, sleeping in closets or floors and most of all, not being loved.

Shade vowed he would work hard and get into college. He never wanted to be a professional hockey player. In truth, he had no clue what he wanted to do professionally. Maybe something in marketing because he always did well in those types of classes. Nonetheless, fate decided he needed to be in the PHL.

"Hey, Shade."

Shade turned to see his good friend, Dag, jogging up to him. "Hey."

"What are you doing here?"

Shade usually came in at the last minute. "Meeting with Cabel," he stated.

"You okay?"

"Sure," he said, almost coldly.

"Want to grab some lunch?"

"Not sure. I'll catch up with you." He rushed away and went through the players' entrance and toward the elevator up to the offices.

As he stepped off, a child's squeal made him freeze. Running toward him was three-year-old Klara Elgin, Nova and Teo's daughter. Her light brown hair, styled in pigtails, bounced wildly. Her pale blue eyes full of delight and happiness.

"Shade." She rushed to him with open arms.

He bent down to pick up the child. It took everything in him to smile. Clay and Klara had been born on the same day, less than a few hours apart.

"Mommy chasing me." Klara's giggles grew as she pointed down the hall.

His heart broke thinking of how he should be chasing his son.

"Hi, Shade." Nova came around the corner. She looked nervously between Klara and him.

He knew they tried to keep Klara away from him because she was a sad reminder for him. Yet somehow, the little girl always seemed to seek him out.

"Hey, Nova," he managed to say with a lump in his throat.

"Shade, you play with me?" Klara asked, fiddling with his collar.

"Not right now. Next time, promise," he told her. Surprisingly his voice remained steady.

"Okay." She hugged his neck tightly. "Love you." She released him and began to wiggle in his arms. He set her feet on the floor, and she bolted down the hall letting her laughter echo bounce off the walls.

"I'm sorry," Nova quickly apologized. "I didn't realize you were going to be here today."

"It's fine. I'm going to see Cabel." Giving her a smile, he rushed away. Today wasn't the day to see that sweet little girl.

Cabel's secretary waved at Shade to let him know Cabel was waiting for him. He pushed open the already ajar door. Cabel Dirks, the Bears' general manager, sat behind his desk, tapping on the keyboard in front of him.

"Morning, Shade." Cabel finally glanced up. "Take a seat over at the table. I'm almost done."

He pulled out a chair around the small table and waited for him. Cabel then came over with a piece of paper.

"Shade." He softly sighed. "Teams are asking for you, but I'm not ready to send you away."

With his hands folded out in front of him, he stared at his fingers and couldn't remember when they started to look old. He was about to turn thirty in a few short weeks.

"You had a great season, Shade." Cabel praised him.

This past season had been one of his best, which surprised him more than anyone. Considering his home life remained in turmoil.

"I am going to assume you've already talked to Jenessa about everything."

He couldn't say out loud that he and his wife have barely spoken to each other over the past three years. He didn't even know if Jenessa remembered his contract with the Bears was about to expire.

"Well, um, Shade…" Cabel stammered since he didn't answer him. "You need to tell me what to do?"

He leaned forward, placing his elbows on the table. Thoughts swirled around his head. Yes, he loved hockey. Yes, he loved his wife. However, right now he felt all he did was cause her pain. Deep down, he needed to leave her. His constant reminder caused her more discomfort, and he was the source.

Taking a deep breath, he found the courage to say, "Trade me."

CHAPTER TWO
Jenessa

Even though the office began to make strides into a paperless world, Jenessa's desk still held several piles of papers, making her feel unsatisfied and stressed at the same time. Work. Her office. This building. All of it took her away from the reality that she called her life.

Her life.

Her life?

Many times since the death of her son, she questioned if it had any true meaning. Or if she should continue it at all. Thoughts of ending it floated in and out of her mind more than once in the past three years, but she never followed through with it.

"Mrs. Wooten."

Jenessa blinked several times trying to focus unsure if she really heard her name or if her mind was playing tricks again.

"Mrs. Wooten?"

"Yes," she finally said, seeing the red light flashing on the phone system.

"The clients are in conference room number one."

"Thank you, Tiffany," she said to her assistant and picked up her iPad.

She took a couple of breaths before she walked out of her office.

Jenessa wanted to be a lawyer ever since she watched *Law and Order* as a child. Her mother thought it was ridiculous. Then again, her mother still lived in the 1950s. She thought women should be at home, barefoot and pregnant, baking pies and cooking dinner as the men went off and conquered the world.

Jenessa never bought that story. Her desires were to change the world for good and by her hand. She never even pictured getting married or having children until she met Shade. Their chance meeting changed her entire world, future, everything. And at the same time she loved it. Shade was her partner, best friend, companion until…

Shaking away her emotions she strolled confidently into the conference room ready to take steps to change the world.

When the meeting ended, Jenessa had a fake smile on her face, something she'd done since returning to work after…

"Mrs. Wooten?"

Turning she saw Tiffany rushing to her. Which meant one thing. "Is my sister in my office?"

Tiffany nodded with a worried expression.

"I'll take care of her." She sighed, making her way back down the hall.

Opening the door to her office, her eyes landed on Mikayla who had her feet on the desk.

"What up, Nes?" Mikayla smiled as she greeted her sister.

"What do you want?" Jenessa didn't want to play any games with her. She needed to get to the point and then leave.

"Lunch," she answered, removing her feet from the desk. "Let's go."

Jenessa rolled her eyes. A trait she and Mikayla had in common, which might be the only one. They really didn't look like sisters at all.

"I don't have time." She set her iPad down on the desk and pointed to the door. "You can go."

"Nope." She stood, moving in front of her. "You and I are going to lunch. Together. Right now."

Crossing her arms, she glared at Mikayla. "And if I said no?"

Smirking, she began to walk backward toward the door, not breaking eye contact and sat on the floor directly in the path of the door.

"Then I'm planting my ass right here until you say yes." Raising one eyebrow, she sent a silent challenge.

Jenessa growled and threw her hands up into the air. She knew she would remain there. Mikayla never backed down. "You're the most childish adult on this planet."

"Great." Mikayla cheered and stood up. "I want Mexican."

Knowing the sooner she got this over with, the sooner Mikayla would leave, and she could get back to work. Grabbing her purse, she barely acknowledged Mikayla as she stormed out of the office and toward the elevator.

The silent treatment continued until the waiter took their drink order. She felt Mikayla's glare, but she ignored it by staring at the menu.

"You can cut the royal bitch act," Mikayla commanded. "I know you're just a regular bitch."

Her words made Jenessa drop the menu. "Just tell me what you want so I can leave."

"Fine." She sat back, crossed her arms, and narrowed her glare. "No more bullshit. I don't fucking care if you never talk to me, but I will not stand idly by and let you cut Shade down like he's a dead tree and you're a chainsaw."

She figured this was the reason for the visit. Mikayla and Shade were closer than actual blood siblings. They'd been that way since their first meeting.

"He's a good man," she continued. "He has put up with all your shit without one ounce of a complaint. If it had been any other man, he would have left your ass years ago. But Shade has been right there for you."

She couldn't argue with her because she was right. Although, she'd never admit it.

"If you don't want to be with him or whatever the fuck is going on with you, then you need to let him go. I told you before, you keep this up, and you'll be alone. Forever."

Mikayla's firm tone made Jenessa freeze in her place. Just as it had when she said it all those weeks ago.

"I don't think you seem to under—"

"Stop." Mikayla held up her hand. "You're right. I don't understand your pain, but Shade does. All these years you two should have been leaning on each other. But you decided to hurt the man whom you love and who loves you."

Tears were trying to creep up, but she knew how to shut them away faster than a vault door.

"Let him go, Jenessa. Because last night, you killed that man with your words deeper than any knife could. Any wife who truly loved her husband would have never ever said it."

Without giving her a chance to defend her actions, or even try to explain, Mikayla got up from the booth, leaving Jenessa alone.

When Jenessa finally made it home after nine o'clock, Shade was sitting at the breakfast bar with several Thai takeout boxes in front of him.

"Hey," he greeted her.

"Hey," she replied as she dropped everything on the kitchen island and opened the fridge, grabbing a bottle of wine and pouring a large glass.

"There's plenty of food for you too." He pointed with

his chopsticks.

Jenessa didn't respond. She took several gulps of the red wine until the glass was emptied. Without saying anything else she walked upstairs to the master bath and went to run water in the tub but stopped when she noticed Shade standing in the doorway.

"No more stalling, Jen. We need to talk. Now."

"Talk." She shrugged, taking a seat at the edge of the tub. Even though he was a tough hockey player, she knew Shade never enjoyed confrontation. He avoided it at all costs.

"I want *you* to talk to me," he stated.

Again, she shrugged. "I have nothing to say."

Studying his face, she noticed his cheeks growing red and a vein in his neck popped out. All signs telling her he was mad. More than mad. Absolutely infuriated.

"Fine." He turned and left her alone.

Her plans for a hot bath to relax were shot to hell. Instead, she went into the bedroom and laid down. Staring at the ceiling, Mikayla's words floated through her mind. Her younger sister was always brighter than she let on. Or Jenessa gave her credit for lately. There were times Mikayla's spontaneous—sometimes reckless—behavior was completely opposite of Jenessa, and it helped balance each other out. Jenessa has always been studious, the planner, the one who never did anything without thinking about from every single angle.

Then Shade came into her life.

The moment they introduced themselves to each other, her world was turned upside down. And she loved every single second of it. Until her world slipped off its axis. No one could understand what she was going through. No one felt the pain that consumed her. Every day she sank further and further into a black hole. She felt her baby kick. She heard his heartbeat. She was his mother. The only one meant to protect him.

And he died because of her.

A hot tear escaped her eye, and she quickly wiped it away. She couldn't cry anymore. It took her a long time to realize that these erratic emotions wouldn't bring back her baby.

Her stomach grumbled, and she remembered there was food downstairs waiting for her. Even though she didn't care about food, she knew a long night of work was ahead of her. When she walked into the kitchen, she saw that Shade had left out everything for her on the bar. She moved it all to the kitchen table. Jenessa could never master the chopsticks like Shade. She stabbed the food still in the takeout container with a fork, opened her laptop, and started working on her motion.

Deep into the research, she buried herself further in the case law, pushing away the reality settling around her. Glancing at the time on her laptop, she couldn't believe the clock read one in the morning.

Hearing the TV still going in the den, she made her way down the hall. Stretched out on the sectional, Shade was fast asleep. Watching him silently for several seconds, she thought about Mikayla's words *again*. She didn't say anything Jenessa hadn't thought over a hundred times in the past three years. Shade was too good for her. She knew it. He was the type of man woman only read about in books. Jaw-dropping good looks, perfectly built body, rough and tough appearance, but a true romantic and gentleman. Pulling the blanket from the back of the sectional, she covered him up and turned off the TV.

After Jenessa changed and laid down in the bed, she did the same thing she had done every night for the past few years. Hoped she'd wake up and it was a dream.

"Mrs. Wooten?"

Jenessa looked up from her laptop screen. "Yes,

Tiffany."

"Um…is there anything else you need? It's almost seven, and my babysitter is close to leaving if I don't get home soon." Tiffany's tiny voice seemed almost scared of her.

"Seven?" She twisted her wrist to see the time. She couldn't believe it. Where had the day gone? "Yes, of course. See you tomorrow."

"It's Friday," Tiffany reminded her.

"Sure. Right." She had completely forgotten what day of the week it was. "Until Monday then."

With a small smile, she rushed out of the office.

Leaning back, she pinched the bridge of her nose. She'd been here for twelve hours and didn't even notice it. Dropping her hand, she took a deep breath and figured she'll finish everything at home.

Jenessa barely remembered driving home and determined she needed more sleep. Pulling into the driveway, she turned off her car and leaned back in the seat. People shouldn't dread going home. It should be welcoming and safe. But she hated coming here. A darkness hung over the house. A thousand times she wanted to run away and say *fuck it* to everything yet somehow she stayed. She stayed because of Shade.

Getting out of the car and gathering her items, Jenessa made her way into the house. Walking in, she placed everything on the kitchen island. Sounds from the den told her he was home and playing video games. A part—a large part—of her told her to go and talk to him, but she ignored that part and pulled out her laptop and work.

As she began to work, trying to ignore the sound of the loud video game in the background, she didn't want to think about the weekend. This meant two whole days trying to avoid Shade. She knew he would start suggesting things to do. It was something he recently started doing again. Pinching the bridge of her nose, again, she quickly tried to think of diversion plans. None of the excuses she thought would work. Shade was smart and would see through her in a heartbeat. He had the ability to read her like an open book.

Finally, she couldn't take the sounds anymore. Slapping her hands down she stood and stormed off to the den. Shade sat in the middle of the sectional, staring straight ahead, not even noticing her.

"Shade!" She stomped her foot, finally gaining his attention.

He jumped slightly. "Hey." He paused the game. "I didn't hear you come in."

"You wouldn't be able to hear a hurricane," she snapped at him.

"I didn't know you were here," he repeated, setting down the controller. "What time is it?"

"Time for you to grow up and stop playing silly games," Jenessa growled, crossing her arms and glaring at him.

Shade scrubbed his face hard with his hands and then looked up at her. "Jen, I'm not in the mood to fight tonight, okay? I've had a long—"

"Don't even say *you* had a long day." She cut him off. "I'm the one who works. You just play hockey." She couldn't explain why she said such a thing, but the words just kept coming out, each hurting him more than the last.

"Jenessa, stop." He stood up. His hard stare caused her to take a step back. Shade would never hurt her, and she knew it, but she couldn't stop hurting him.

"No, I will not. What have you done? Worked out? Eat? Hang out with Jarvis, Dag, and Edgar? Wow, sounds like a productive day." She spun on her heel to go back down the hall.

Shade followed her. "Stop acting like I don't do anything around here."

"Oh, do you?" She called over her shoulder, not looking at him.

"What do you want from me, Jenessa? What?" He

raised his voice causing her to stop and face him. She didn't answer him. "I'm trying everything to get us back to normal."

"You don't think I'm *normal*?"

He tossed his hands in the air. "Stop twisting my words, Counselor. You know what I mean."

She did but avoided saying it. Instead, she turned on the defensive. "You know what, Shade, if you're not happy with our *normal* life, then just fucking leave."

Even though they have had so many issues the past few years, neither have left nor even said the words.

Until now.

Their eyes remained locked on each other. Jenessa's heart raced, tears burned behind her eyes. She couldn't take the words back. They hung in the air between them. The only sound she heard was the ringing in her ears.

"You win, Jenessa. You win," Shade spoke first, nodding and dropping his eyes to the floor. "I don't know what else to do. I've tried everything, but I can't do this anymore. I love you with every single part of my being, but I can't do *this* anymore. So…you win."

She stood frozen in the hallway as Shade moved around her. Her feet wouldn't move. She listened as he went upstairs. She couldn't hear what was happening, but she knew. Deep down, she knew he was packing a bag. Still standing in the same spot, his heavy feet came back down the stairs, his keys jingled, and the front door slammed shut.

Shade was gone.

CHAPTER THREE
Shade

Waking up after a very restless night's sleep, Shade couldn't believe it'd been just over twelve hours since he left the house. Nothing felt right.

After stepping out of the house, he sat in his truck for fifteen minutes—or longer—hoping Jenessa would come out and get him. Tell him she didn't want him to leave, and they'd work it out.

But that never happened.

Then he drove around, unsure of where to go or what to do. He never felt this lost. As time continued to pass, he ended up at a hotel. He couldn't drive all night, and he didn't want to bother any of his teammates by asking them to let him crash on their couch. When he checked in the young lady behind the counter clearly knew who he was and gave him a smile when she handed him the key card. Honestly, he didn't care if anyone noticed him right now. Once he made it into the hotel room, he just laid on the bed.

When the sun had risen the next day he sat up, looking around. What should he do next? Obviously, he couldn't live in a hotel room. What about all his stuff at the house? Should he get it today? Should he wait? Had she called?

Questions raced and spun faster and faster in his mind to the point they gave him a headache. Rubbing his temple, he struggled to get out of the bed and head toward the shower. He thought the hot water would clear his mind. In truth, it didn't help at all.

After finishing his shower, he didn't bother to look in the mirror. He knew his five o'clock shadow was poking through his skin. Instead, he just slid into a pair of jeans and a T-shirt. Taking a seat at the small table in the room, he sighed. Shade hadn't felt this despair since he was a child, bouncing from foster home to foster home. He hated this feeling more than anything.

Knock. Knock.

Shade didn't even have to look through the peephole. He just opened the door, and there stood Mikayla, with Jarvis by her side, staring back at him.

"What are you doing here?"

He texted her when he arrived at the hotel to let her know where he was and if Jenessa wanted to contact him. Which he knew she wouldn't.

"I'm here to talk." She strolled in and Jarvis was on her heels.

"Mikayla, I love you, but today's not the day." He shut the door and followed her further into the room.

Turning, she gave him a small sad smile. "I know, but you're not going to stay in a hotel, Shade. You can't."

"You can come stay with me," Jarvis suggested.

Immediately, he shook his head. "No. You have Joy there and Mikayla stays over a lot. I won't intrude on you."

"Joy is with Jackson most of the time, and you've already lived with Mikayla, so you know all her issues," Jarvis joked, causing her to roll her eyes.

Shade sat down and shook his head. "I'm not sure what to do," he mumbled, half to himself and half to them.

Mikayla bent down in front of him. "You're going to pack your shit, get in your truck, and go to Jarvis's place. We'll grab breakfast on the way back and meet you there."

He knew he could argue with her, but he'd never win. Mikayla, like Jenessa, would always win an argument.

"All right." He gave in.

Jarvis and Mikayla left, and Shade repacked the few items he had taken out of his bag. He checked out, got into his truck, and drove downtown to Jarvis's condo. He'd been on the approved list for many years, so he just nodded to the doorman and went up the elevator. He knew the code to get in and shut off the alarm. Shade had kept an eye on the condo when Jarvis traveled for whatever modeling job he had at the time. Going straight to the third bedroom, he dropped his bag on the bed and sat down.

"I'm homeless," Shade said to the empty room. Technically, he wasn't because he had money in the bank to get a place of his own without any real worry. He just didn't want to because he would be traded soon enough. He decided he'll give money to Jarvis for letting him stay here until he was off to his new team.

"We're here." Mikayla's voice carried through the condo.

Shade hadn't moved, nor did he know how long he'd been sitting there. He knew they were just being kind to him but food didn't sound good at all to him.

"Hey."

Raising his head, he saw her standing in the doorway.

"Come and eat."

"I'm not hungry."

"Don't do that." Mikayla came into the room and sat next to him. "You can't hide from this. You have to move on."

"I'm not hiding. I don't know how to move on from Jen," he countered. "I have done everything for us. Everything. I don't know how to live without her in my life. I don't know how to breathe without her. I don't know what to do."

He stared at Mikayla and saw the shocked and sad

expression on her face. Then he felt the hot tears on his cheeks. Turning away from her, he wiped them away. Only in private would he cry, but here he sat on the bed with his sister-in-law as the tears fell.

"Shade, I don't want you to leave Jenessa, but it's what you *have* to do for her to see the truth."

He didn't say anything.

"She's different and you know it as well as I do. She has to hit rock bottom before she realizes all that she has and comes back to you."

"And what if she doesn't ever come back?" He buried his face in his hands.

"She will. Give her time."

He hated that sentence more than any other. *Time.* That was a word with no definition. How much time? How much time before they're back together and being happy again?

"Let's take one minute at a time," Mikayla suggested. "Let's eat and then we'll decide what's next. Deal?"

He knew she was right. Slowly, he nodded and stood up. "Okay. Let's eat."

After breakfast, Shade went back to the bedroom and remained there for the rest of the day and night. He tried to sleep, tried to watch TV, tried to do anything but think of the pain he felt. Mikayla left him be, as did Jarvis. They didn't even bother him for lunch or dinner. He just stayed away from them all, and they let him.

As the sun came up the next day, it had been over twenty-four hours since he'd talked to Jenessa. Since their first meeting, he'd never gone this long without talking to her. Even when they were long-distance from each other, they'd talked every day.

He shaved and showered in the en suite bathroom

before emerging from the bedroom. He quietly made his way into the kitchen where Jarvis sat at the breakfast bar.

"She's not here," he told Shade, answering his unasked question. "She's working today."

"Is it bad to say I'm relieved?" He grabbed the orange juice container and poured himself a cup.

"Nah, even I need a break from her. She wears me out," he confessed. "What's your plans for today?"

He leaned against the counter. "I have no idea."

"Come work out with us," he suggested. "Camp is about to start. You don't want to lose your spot."

"I'm being traded," Shade blurted out.

"What?" Jarvis's jaw dropped. "What the fuck are you talking about?"

"I asked Cabel the other day to trade me. My contract is up, and I can't stay here without Jenessa," he admitted to Jarvis.

"You're lying, right? This is a bad joke or dream or something," Jarvis began to ramble.

"It's not," Shade told him seriously. "I don't know where I'm going, but it's somewhere nowhere near Manchester."

"Damn," he breathed. "I hate to lose you, bro."

Shade had no reply because he hated to leave. Manchester was his home. His first real home. "Let's go workout," he said, hoping all these feelings and emotions would leave him with each droplet of sweat.

Jarvis drove them both to the Bears' arena. Janan and Nova, the owners of the New Hampshire Bears, the Manchester Cats, the professional baseball team, and the Concord Rams, the professional football team, had made sure there was a state-of-the-art gym for the players in the arenas that they could use anytime. The Bears' players took full advantage of it.

When they walked in, Dag Limon, Edgar Hopp, Bas Zorn, Zerrick Justice, and Walker Lange were already there. After everyone greeted each other, Shade hit the treadmill first. He didn't run hard, just a steady jog to get his heart rate up a bit. He couldn't push himself because he didn't want to hurt himself or get sick since he'd not really eaten.

After about twenty minutes, he hit the free weights until the sweat burned his eyes, and his muscles screamed for him to stop. His body almost collapsed when he put down the weights and went over to the fridge for something to drink. Edgar had been sitting on a bench, and Shade joined him, twisting the top off the bottle.

"You left her, didn't you?" Edgar kept his question low.

"How did you know?" Shade asked shocked. He knew Mikayla and Jarvis wouldn't tell anyone.

"It's written all over your face," he told him point-blank.

"The night before last," he confessed. "She told me to leave and…I did."

"Shit," he breathed. "I hate to hear that, Shade. I really do. I know you wanted to work it out, but maybe this is a good thing."

"Good? This isn't good. This is the furthest thing from good," he barked at his friend.

"You have every right to be pissed, but now you can move on."

Shade had no intention of ever moving on. His love and soul belonged to Jenessa and no one else. Even when he moves to whatever city he'll be traded to, he'd never find a love like they had.

"I'm going to wait for Jarvis outside." Shade stood up and left the gym.

He wasn't going to wait for Jarvis. Instead, when he stepped into the sunlight and warm air, he summoned an Uber and texted Jarvis to let him know he left.

Back at the condo, he took another shower and realized he'd need to run to the drugstore and purchase some items. He could go to the house and get them, but he couldn't face her. Checking his phone for the hundredth time, Jenessa still hadn't called or texted him. It was more continuing proof the marriage was over.

At the drugstore, he strolled aimlessly through the aisles, not looking at anything in particular but tossing items he needed into his basket. He could almost hear Jenessa bitching because he didn't have a list. She always went into the store, purchased the items on the list, and checked out.

When he finished and went back to the condo, he stayed in his room watching TV until Mikayla pushed open the door without knocking.

"Get up, now." She roughly yanked on his arm. "You're not going to waste away in this room."

"You're about to pull my arm out of the socket." He jerked away from her grasp.

"I brought food home and even if I have to shove it down your throat, you will eat it." She glared at him.

He never could explain it, but Mikayla always had a commanding personality. Even more so than Jenessa. "You win."

"Oh, I know I do." She smarted off back at him and continued to stare him down until he began making his way to the door.

Once in the kitchen, Jarvis was already at the breakfast bar with several takeout containers around them. Mikayla pointed for him to sit down, and he did, and then she sat in between the guys. She placed three containers in front of him. Her glare softened when he began placing food on his plate.

They ate quietly for several minutes before Mikayla began telling them about her day. She was currently working for one of the world's leading designers helping to create an accessory line of costume jewelry. Shade listened to her but really didn't process the words a lot. Even though he was glad she was working on an outstanding career, his mood wouldn't let him be happy for her.

After he ate about half of the food, he got up without saying anything and went back to the bedroom. He had the TV on, but it was purely for the white noise and nothing else. He sat in a chair that was facing the window. The sun had already set, and he just stared out at the Manchester skyline. People were moving about their happy lives and what about him? He had nothing. No real home. The love of his life was gone. And he was to be traded soon.

A knock on the door brought him back to the present.

"Come in, Mikayla," he said not looking at the door.

"She's much hotter than me," Jarvis said, stepping into the room.

Turning, he saw his friend. "Sorry. I figured she was going to give me the third degree."

"Give it time. She will, but I told her I'd talk to you first." He came over to him and sat on the edge of the bed.

"Sorry, I ditched you. I just had to leave," he began to explain.

"I get it. I do. Your heart is broken, and it seems like there's nothing in this world to fix it."

Shade glanced at his friend and then back at the window. "Something like that."

"I know you want to be traded, but I wish you'd reconsider."

"I can't stay here without her," he answered quickly. Being in Manchester would only feel like home if they were together.

"I know. I thought I'd ask." Jarvis stood up and touched his shoulder. "You can stay here for as long as you need."

"Thanks," Shade said with sincerity as Jarvis headed out the room.

Looking back out the window, he wondered how long he'd be here before he was traded.

CHAPTER FOUR
Jenessa

Time seemed to speed by but as Jenessa stared at her laptop, it moved at a snail's pace. She should have been at the office, but for the past several days, she hadn't left the house. Slamming the laptop shut she moved from the kitchen table into the den. Wrapping herself up in the blanket that sat on the back of the sectional, she inhaled Shade's scent.

For the millionth time in the past few days, tears silently ran down her cheeks as she laid there. She felt a hole in her soul and had since hearing the front door close when Shade left. She'd spent the weekend in bed, barely leaving it. Even when Mikayla tried to make her get up, she remained frozen under the sheets.

She thought about turning on the TV but couldn't find the energy or care to pick up the remote. What did it matter? All there was were happy couples and perfect lives. The real world or real problems were never portrayed on TV. At least not the way they really turned out. What did she care? Her life was nothing now. He hadn't even called or texted her.

One thought that continued to pop into her head was if he was with someone else. Was he? She never figured

Shade to be a cheater, but then again, she never thought he'd leave her. Now look at her.

When the front door opened, she sat up thinking Shade came back. Then her heart sank when she saw Mikayla's turned-up nose.

"Holy shit. You stink."

"Go away." Jenessa groaned, falling back down onto the sectional.

"I probably should because you're burning my eyes, and I'll never be able to get rid of this smell out of my clothes." Mikayla waved her hand in front of her face. "You need to shower."

"Leave me alone," Jenessa ordered with a firm tone.

"Nope. I'm going to throw you into a shower, shove food down your throat, then go home and burn these clothes. So, hurry up." She snapped her fingers at her older sister.

"Weren't you the one who told me I'd be alone?" A surge of anger pulsed through her. "Why aren't you gloating? Or dancing a jig?"

"Did you just ask me why I wasn't dancing a *jig*?" Mikayla questioned.

"Yes. Yes, I am. You've treated me like shit for a long time telling me about this moment." Jenessa jumped to her feet. "Well, here you go." She held out her arms. Waiting for several seconds for her sister to say anything.

Mikayla stepped up to her with a sad expression. "I love you. You're my sister. As much as I want to yell from the rooftops I'm right, I can't do it. You and Shade are broken and the only way to fix you both is for you both to realize your worth. Your worth to yourself and to each other."

Jenessa said nothing. There were many times when Mikayla got under her skin, but other times she became the sound of reason.

"Shade isn't broken." Jenessa put up her defensive walls, making sure no one saw her true weakness.

"Yes, he is. You can stop pretending you're not. Because if you weren't upset about his leaving then you'd be showered, makeup done, hair perfect, and in clothes that didn't appear to have been picked out of the dumpster. Oh, and your eyes wouldn't be puffy and bloodshot," Mikayla called her out.

Arguing would have been pointless. Like her, Mikayla wouldn't stop until she won. The difference, Jenessa knew when to throw in the towel.

At least, sometimes.

"Seriously, get showered. I brought food." Mikayla's words came out like a commander ordering his troops.

For some reason, Jenessa's body followed Mikayla's orders. She moved off the sectional, dropped the blanket behind her, made her way to the stairs, up to the bedroom, and into the master bath. The cool water shocked her skin, causing it to tingle. She didn't deserve hot water. She began scrubbing away the body odor and several days' worth of sadness and despair.

Stepping out, her skin glowed red from the harsh, rough cleaning she just gave herself. Patting herself dry she slipped into a pair of sweats and a T-shirt. No makeup. Hair still dripping wet. None of which she cared about at the moment. Going back downstairs, Mikayla had a large veggie pizza sitting in the middle of the kitchen table with two glasses of Hi-C Fruit Punch.

"Let's eat." She sat down.

Jenessa couldn't lie. The smell of pizza made her mouth water and stomach growl. "I'd figured you make mac and cheese." She heard the harshness of her tone. She hoped it would send Mikayla away, so she could go back to being alone.

"Nope. We needed serious carbs tonight. Pizza will hit the mark." She pulled a slice off and put it on the plate in front of Jenessa.

Picking it up, she took a small bite. She had to hold back the moan because she didn't want Mikayla to think she was right.

"Are you going back to the office? Or are you going to quit yet?" she questioned her sister, grabbing a slice for herself.

"Why would I quit my job, Kay?"

"Because you hate it and you're using it as a crutch," she answered the rhetorical question.

"I do not. It's a very rewarding job," Jenessa countered.

"No, it's not. You keep saying that because you *want* to believe it. In truth, it sucks and it's sucking your soul dry. So, when are you going to quit?"

Jenessa ignored her and went back to eating her pizza.

"Shade will need to come by and get his stuff."

This statement made her freeze midbite. She knew it would be coming, but it still shocked her. Shade taking his stuff out of the house would finalize her fear. He'll never come back. "Sure. Whatever."

Mikayla rolled her eyes. "Really? You're going to play the tough girl card?"

"I'm not playing any card," she defensively snapped.

"Well, your bubbly attitude says differently. In case you didn't know." Mikayla went back to her food, still staring at her.

Jenessa put her head down, then she picked at the veggie toppings, only eating a piece here and there. Finally, she gave up. She didn't want to be in the same room as Mikayla anymore. She got up from the table and went up to the bedroom. Slamming the door shut she hoped her sister would take the hint and leave her alone.

Curling up on her side, she reached for Shade's pillow and tucked it in her arms. Again, she inhaled his scent. He never wore anything overpowering. It always smelled fresh and minty. While growing up, Jenessa always loved the scent of spearmint and when they'd first met, it was an aroma that hung in the air between them. Closing her eyes, she thought about her and Shade's first meeting. Fate had set them up.

Jenessa grew up in Buffalo, New York and loved the city life. When it came time to apply for college, she never thought of moving too far away. In truth, she didn't want to leave Mikayla with her parents without having any 'back-up' as they called it. Jenessa loved college life. She made many friends, stayed at the top of her class, and networked her ass off. She knew she needed to if she wanted to get into law school. She overloaded herself, but since she considered herself a workaholic, she knew she could handle it.

Then one night, a friend wanted to meet up for coffee at a small hole-in-the-wall diner. Jenessa always prided herself on being there for her friends. As she sat at the booth and ordered some coffee for herself, she smelled something minty. Turning to her left, she saw a handsome guy, around her age, sitting alone at the table next to her booth. She tried not to stare but continued to glance at him several more times throughout her time there.

After twenty minutes of waiting, she got on her cell phone and called her friend. When she answered, she told her that she was back with her boyfriend and everything was fine. Jenessa ended the call and had "apparently" sighed loudly, thus gaining Shade's attention.

"Stood up?"

She shrugged. "Something like it." She looked at him. "What about you?"

"Just a night by myself," he answered with a smile.

Then Jenessa asked the one question which would change her life forever. "Would you like to join me?" She just blurted it out, unsure why she asked this stranger to join her.

"I'd love to." He quickly moved from his table to her booth, sitting across from her.

Immediately, they began talking. Not one second of awkwardness passed between them. Jenessa felt like they were old friends. She told him about Mikayla, college life, and her dreams of being a lawyer. He told her about hockey and his future of possibly being in the PHL. Even if it didn't work out, he'd have his college degree in business, and he thought about getting his MBA and working for a sports advertising company.

Shade paid for everything when they realized how late it was and even walked her to her car. They'd exchanged numbers and before she even made it back to her dorm, Shade had called and asked her to go out.

From that point on, they talked or saw each other every single day.

Jenessa told Tiffany she'd be working from home again, and Tiffany told her the partners weren't too thrilled about it. Truthfully, Jenessa could not care less. She'd been thinking of leaving the firm. Again, Mikayla was right. She didn't feel fulfilled with her job anymore. She sat at the kitchen table, laptop open and should be typing up a motion, but in truth, she'd not typed one word. Mikayla had left the pizza, and Jenessa grabbed a slice before going into the living room and sitting in the middle of the couch. Eating the cold piece of pizza reminded her of her college days when she and Shade would eat at her apartment.

When she heard the front door keypad, she figured Mikayla had decided to come back and pick up where they left off last night. To her shock, Shade opened the door. Thankfully, she didn't have a mouth full of food when their eyes connected.

"Um...hey," Shade spoke first and shut the door. "I thought you'd be at work."

"I'm working from home," she explained, hating that she looked like a wreck at the moment.

"Okay." The tension hung in the air. "I just came to grab some clothes and things."

His words broke her heart even more. "Sure. Right." Quickly, she moved to the kitchen and away from him.

She couldn't watch him remove any of his things from the house. Their house. The life they built together. He was leaving. Proving to her the marriage was really over. They'd been together for over ten years, married almost eight, and it was all ending. Holding onto the counter, she didn't want him to see her cry. Actually, she couldn't believe she had any tears left. She'd figured her tear ducts would have dried up by now.

Unsure of how long she'd been standing there, she eventually heard Shade coming down the stairs and into the kitchen. A thud indicated a heavy bag being dropped onto the floor. The smell of mint filled the air.

"Um, I just took clothes and personal stuff."

She heard the crack in his voice. Still she couldn't face him. "Okay."

"I'm over at Jarvis's place for now. You know, until…" He trailed off.

Until he found a new house. Until their divorce was finalized. Until he found a new girlfriend and started a new life.

"Sure. See ya," she snapped.

"Right. Okay. See ya."

She knew he wasn't moving because she could still feel his eyes on her. It felt like forever before she heard him pick up the bag and leave the house again. Once the door shut, the tears fell. They didn't last long this time because she wouldn't allow it. She refused to be some weepy female. Even though she'd done it for the past several days, she was over it. He had begun to move on and so would she.

Even if she didn't want to.

Shortly after Shade left, Jenessa made the decision that she wasn't going to work at all today. It had become pointless because her brain had no ability to focus. She knew she couldn't stay in the house for one more second. The walls were beginning to close in on her and cabin fever would shortly follow. However, she didn't know what to do. She thought about shopping or maybe deep cleaning the house. Neither of which sounded appealing.

Then she randomly walked around the house and began opening the hall closets. In one, she saw her yoga mat and bag. Bending down, she picked it up and wondered when was the last time she'd done yoga. She went to yoga all throughout college and law school. She even did meditation classes. It wasn't until she was eight months pregnant when she stopped her prenatal yoga classes. Even though she felt flexible, it became harder for her. Thinking about it more and more, she realized how much she missed yoga and how much she loved going.

Reaching for her phone, she searched to see if the same yoga studio she'd gone to before had any classes going on right now. It did and she quickly got ready and headed downtown to the studio.

Jenessa actually felt nervous walking into the class. She'd only been around co-workers and Shade and Mikayla since her baby died. Occasionally, she did try to go to Bears' events, but she couldn't tolerate it. One of the owners, Nova Long, gave birth to a daughter the exact same day Jenessa had Clay. Jenessa would never be mean or blame an innocent child for her heartache. She just couldn't handle seeing the child thriving when hers was gone.

As the instructor started, Jenessa quickly realized, she was completely out of shape. She tried to stretch herself as far as her body would allow but couldn't do it like she used to. Sweat formed around her forehead and her back, and it made her skin clammy. At the end of the session, the instructor did five minutes of meditation.

Taking deep breaths and centering herself, Jenessa cleared her mind. She didn't feel at peace. However, she was able to empty her thoughts.

"Now, focus on your one true desire," the instructor said.

Shade flashed into her mind. He had been sitting on the floor with baby toys all around. Even though she couldn't see the baby's face because it was facing away from her, she could hear the cooing and laughter. She never doubted Shade would have been the world's best father.

When the session ended and Jenessa opened her eyes, she felt the tears. She rushed to wipe them away not wanting anyone to see them. All in all, she felt a little better. Rolling up her mat, she already made the decision to come back tomorrow.

"Jenessa?"

She looked over her shoulder to see Greer Hopp coming up to her. "Hi, Greer," she greeted her.

"How have you been?"

Doing a quick once over, she felt like a slug next to Greer. Greer Hopp was the den mother of the New Hampshire Bears and wife to Edgar Hopp. She also owned and ran an extremely successful event planning company. Not to mention she was the perfect Pinterest mother and looked like she belonged on the cover of Vogue. Her beautiful brown shiny hair sat high in a ponytail. Even without makeup the woman didn't have a blemish on her face.

"I'm okay." She gathered the rest of her items, trying not to divulge any more information than she needed to. Unsure of what Shade had told everyone.

"Really? Because, no offense, you look like hell."

Leave it to Greer to be honest and sweet about it at the same time.

"How about we head over to the juice bar and chat?"

She wanted to turn her down and go home. However, something, deep down, told her to go and have a drink with her. "Sure. Why not?"

Together they walked next door to the juice bar. Jenessa didn't want to stand there in silence, so she asked about the business. Greer began to tell her about some of the events she was currently planning. Jenessa had always been impressed with Greer having her own business. She'd thought about opening her own practice many years ago, but the moment passed time and time again.

Once they had their drinks, they found a small table near the window. Greer had an expression as if she wanted to ask the big questions.

"Go ahead and ask." She gave her permission. When Jenessa and Shade first arrived in New Hampshire, Greer and Edgar were their first friends and opened their homes to them many times when they were searching for a home. When Clay died, Greer had been the first from the Bears' family to come to Jenessa's side.

"How are you doing, for real?"

Jenessa took a deep breath and said, "Shitty."

Greer waited for her to continue.

"Shade left." Jenessa heard a small gasp come from across the table.

"Are you okay?" Greer took her hand, not seeming shocked by her words.

"Yes. No. I don't know," she answered in a rush, truly unsure how she felt.

"When did this happen?"

"Last week."

"Why didn't you call? I would have come over."

Nodding, she knew she would have been there in a heartbeat. "I know, but I needed to be alone."

"I can understand." Greer gave her hand a soft squeeze before releasing it. "Is there anything I can do?"

Jenessa shrugged. "I don't know. I don't even know what to do."

"I can't imagine what you're going through. I'm here for anything. Even if it's to listen." Greer gave her a friendly smile.

"You know I only have Mikayla now. Well, that's if she's talking to me." Jenessa's eye roll was meant to be for herself not Greer.

"Shade loves you Jenessa. Could this just be temporary?"

"No." She shook her head. "He came and got some stuff today."

"Have you talked to him?"

Again, she shook her head. A bit embarrassed admitting to it.

"How come?" Greer's shocked tone couldn't be hidden. "I truly can't believe this is what Shade wants."

Not having an answer for her, she didn't say anything and just stared out the window. Greer took the hint and didn't ask any other questions. The women sat at the table, drinking their juice in silence.

Finally, Greer asked, "Would you like to be my yoga partner? We can meet up tomorrow."

Jenessa already knew she was coming back. However, it would be nice to have a female to hang out with. "Sure, I'd like   that."

CHAPTER FIVE
Shade

"You're such an ass." Jarvis pushed on Shade's shoulder.

"Don't be mad because I can do more chin-ups than you," Shade joked. Even though he didn't feel like being in a fun mood, he liked beating Jarvis.

Normally there were many players in the weight room. Today, it was just Jarvis, Edgar, Jackson, and Shade. Jackson Plumley had been the Bears' least favorite player, especially after last season. Nonetheless, he was trying to win back everyone's trust and respect. Jarvis hated Jackson the most. Mainly because his sister, Joy, was sort-of seeing Jackson. They all knew it.

"Let's grab some lunch, guys," Edgar announced. "Jackson, wanna join in?"

"Sure," he said but glanced at Jarvis. Almost as if waiting to see what he had to say. Jarvis just ignored him and grabbed a towel.

"I'll drive," Edgar volunteered.

"No," they all answered in unison. Any person who knew Edgar knew never to drive with him because he was the worst driver.

"You all have been listening to Greer," he grumbled.

"Fine, I won't drive. Shade, that leaves you to be the chauffeur."

"Fine," Shade said, grabbing his gym bag. "Jackson, ride with us." He didn't see the point of making the poor guy ride alone. Jarvis would just have to deal with it or drive himself. He didn't say anything as they all piled into Shade's truck. They decided on Mexican, and Shade started driving to their favorite restaurant.

The guys chatted about the upcoming season. Shade joined in the conversation, even though his mind really wasn't in it. It had been four days since he last saw Jenessa at the house. Neither has spoken to each other. He'd picked up his phone a number of times and started to call her or send her a text, but he never followed through. What would be the point? She couldn't even look at him at the house.

Walking into the restaurant, they found a booth out of the way of the crowded lunch rush. They didn't need to look at a menu when the waitress came. They ordered a round of waters, a large plate of nachos, and two chicken fajita platters. When the waitress left, Edgar told Shade about Jenessa.

"She and Greer have been yoga-ing together."

Shade turned up his nose. Not at the fact Jenessa had been going to yoga because she used to do it all the time but from the adjective he used. "That's not a word."

"You get my point." He smirked. "Anyway, she's okay but not really. At least according to Greer."

"What do you mean?" His concern level jumped to maximum.

"She misses you, loser," Jarvis translated for him. "And she wants you back."

"No...she doesn't want me back." Shade sighed. Unsure of what else to say, the guys continued to stare at him, waiting for him to say more. "Even though I want my marriage to work more than anything, there's nothing else I can do."

The waitress returned with their drinks, and it gave him a moment to compose his thoughts. Knowing Jenessa wasn't doing well broke his heart even more. If that were possible.

"I know I'm not one to add my opinion," Jackson spoke up. "Have you thought about therapy?"

He sighed. Not out of frustration, just exhaustion. "Neither Jenessa nor I would go to a stranger, sit on a couch and discuss our feelings. Not going to happen."

"Then what *is* your plan?" Edgar asked.

Shade said nothing.

"I think the big question is, do you have a plan?" Jarvis countered.

Again, words didn't come to him. He simply sat there.

"Neither one of those are right," Jackson's chimed in again. "Do *you* want to have a plan?"

He stared at his teammate. The question was legit, and Shade's heart screamed yes, but his head couldn't comprehend the words. Even though he sat there quietly, he knew the answer. "I love my wife. I don't care if it sounds emotional or whatever. I love her. We're meant to be together."

"Then why aren't you fighting?" Edgar picked up a chip, dipping it into the salsa.

"Because she doesn't want me to. She let me go," he explained.

"You're full of shit," Jarvis grumbled.

Shade opened his mouth but stopped when their food arrived. As they ate Edgar changed the subject to discussing the upcoming hockey season. Shade welcomed the new topic. His mental state couldn't handle any more talks about Jenessa and their marriage. He thought Edgar did it on purpose.

When they finished and paid, Shade drove everyone back to the arena and their respective vehicles. Once alone, he began to drive toward his home. Well, Jenessa's home. The truck practically made its way over there without any assistance from him, or at least it seemed like it. However, he had no clue why. Before turning on the street, he drove past it and made his way to the condo.

Do you want to have a plan?

Jackson's question bounced around in his mind, and he tried to process it. A simple question with a lot of meaning behind it. He tried many, many times to make his marriage work and nothing helped. Nothing he did or said seemed to bring Jenessa back to the light. The light of their love, their relationship, and their future. She wanted none of it.

She hadn't even contacted him.

Strolling into the condo, he went straight for the bedroom he'd been keeping himself locked up in without actually locking the door. He dropped into the chair facing the window. The sun hung high in the clear sky. A warm September day was spread out in front of him, and he didn't even care. This would have been a perfect day to go for a long run. Something he and Jenessa would do together, but now he sat here…

Alone.

He never thought he would be alone. They were supposed to be together forever. He lingered on the word 'forever'. A memory came flooding back into his mind. One he hadn't thought of in such a long time.

Shade had three obsessions. One, Jenessa. Two, hockey. And three, the one most people didn't understand or even believe, country music. Especially from the 1990s. Anytime a teammate figured out his love for country music, they constantly made fun of him. It caused him to have a wide variety of nicknames throughout his years, but he didn't care.

He had taken Jenessa to a concert in a small venue for an up-and-coming singer. It was their third official date. They had talked every single day since they met but finding time between classes, hockey, and studying, it had been hard to be together. He always craved being around her. He couldn't explain it, but he felt pain from being away from Jenessa.

When he told her to dress 'bar' casual for their date, she told him not to surprise her because she hated surprises. He told her the truth and felt nervous putting the idea out there. Jenessa didn't shy away from it. Even though country music hadn't been her favorite type of music, she remained open to the idea.

Jenessa was only twenty and unable to legally drink. Shade never thought of himself as a big drinker, only the occasional beer now and then. He had no qualms with drinking pop with her during the concert. As long as he was with her, nothing else mattered.

When the music started, the venue was crowded and everyone was standing. Shade had put Jenessa in front of him. He held her close with her back pressed against his chest. She swayed to the music, unconsciously rubbing against him. He tried to keep his hard-on at bay, but his cock twitched more often than not.

When the show ended, they walked out hand-in-hand, and he'd suggested grabbing some food. He asked because he wanted to spend more time with her. She kindly declined with the excuse of having to study. Not wanting to force her, he agreed and took her back to her apartment.

They remained outside in his car, steaming up the windows from their passionate kissing.

"I enjoyed myself tonight," she said.

"I enjoy myself every time we talk or are with each other."

Jenessa rolled her eyes. "Are you thinking that line is going to get you in my bed?"

"No, because I don't need a cheesy line to get in bed with you. I'm in love with you and when, or if, we ever go to bed together, it's because of our love."

Her mouth dropped. Shade knew exactly what he said and didn't regret a single word. He loved her and knew it after their first meeting.

"I'm falling for you as well," she replied.

Shade never thought he would ever have someone love him. He never felt love in his life until Jenessa. She completed him, in every possible way.

No, they were apart. Now, they weren't talking. Now, they were over.

No, his love didn't diminish. He would still give his life

for her, but he didn't know how to fix their relationship and marriage.

Grabbing his laptop off the nightstand, he opened it to the search engine. He hated to type the words, but he did.

Divorce attorneys.

He couldn't believe how many came up. Immediately, he felt overwhelmed. Where would he start? Who did he know that could even help him? He already knew he wanted to give everything to Jenessa. He only wanted to get the rest of his clothes and personal items from the house.

"What the fuck?"

Shade jumped at the sound of Mikayla's raised voice.

"What are you doing?" She glared down at him. "Are you serious?"

"Kay, you know it's time. I can't hold off the inevitable." He closed the laptop and glanced up at her.

"She just needs time." Her tone lowered, and she sat down on the side of the bed. "I know her. You know her. She's still processing everything."

Shaking his head, he didn't know what to say.

"You know this," she reiterated with a firmer tone. "You have to keep fighting for her."

Closing his eyes, he dropped his head. "I have fought. I have fought so damn hard. I don't know if I have the strength to fight anymore. Not to mention, she's not even contacted me. She doesn't want me anymore."

As he said the words, they cut deeper into his broken heart. He didn't know he could feel any more pain, but here it was.

"Please, Shade, for me," his sister-in-law begged. "Don't do anything. I know she'll contact you."

"Really?" he slightly snapped. Normally, he'd never lose it with anyone but anger was building up inside him. "If she loved me so damn much, why did she let me go?"

Mikayla's expression softened into a deeper sadness. "You both have been through a lot together. I don't want to see either of you throw in the towel when you're meant to be together."

At one time, he believed it too. Hell, he wanted it still. If she called him right now, he'd race over to her. He'd run if he had to. She was his soul.

"She doesn't love me anymore. Maybe she loves me but not the way it was before Clay's death. I have done everything I could possibly think of to show her how much I love her, and I'd be there for her. What did I get in return? Nothing. I was in pain too. I cried too. I yelled too. Who was there for me? Who helped me through my grief?" He felt the burn of the tears threatening to fall, but he stopped them.

"Promise me, you'll give her just a little more time," Mikayla begged.

"Fine," he said deadpan. However, this time, he couldn't keep his word. "I need to be alone, Mikayla."

Standing up, she stepped over to him and placed a hand on his shoulder, giving it a small squeeze. "I love you, Shade. I know it might not mean much, but I will always be here for you."

He nodded. He knew how much Mikayla loved him, and he loved her.

She did leave the bedroom and after a moment, his nerves calmed. Opening his laptop again, he stared at the screen. Clicking on a few links, he read a few reviews from previous clients. Nothing seemed to be jumping out at him. All the words began to run together. He closed it again and placed it on the bed. He'd have to worry about it another day.

Shade stretched out on the bed, turning on the TV. He wanted to do something mindless in hope to clear his mind and body of the erratic emotions pulsing through him. He doubted the 90s sitcom reruns would help him, but at this point, anything would be worth trying.

He sat through several episodes before a knock on the door came. "Mikayla, I'm not in the mood," he shouted.

"It's not Mikayla."

The voice on the other side of the door made him jump to his feet, shut off the TV, and quickly open the door. "Hello."

Standing outside his bedroom were his bosses, Janan Long-Baer and Nova Long. The owners of the New Hampshire Bears. Neither of them looked happy.

"We need to have a meeting," Janan said, pushing her way in.

She had always been the alpha of the owners, and Nova was the brains. Oliver Matthews, their godfather and previous owner, knew exactly who would be best for the team when he retired.

"We just need to speak with you for a few moments," Nova clarified, stepping into the room.

"Of course." He shut the door, suddenly becoming nervous. He didn't know how they knew he was at Jarvis's place nor why they were there. Certainly, it had to do with his trade. "What do you want to talk about?"

"You and your stupid idea of being traded," Janan snapped at him, crossing her arms.

"She means, we'd like to talk about other options for you not involving you leaving the Bears," again, Nova spoke.

"Look—"

"Nope." Janan cut him off. "We're going first. Sit down." She took the chair and pointed to the bed. He and Nova sat on the side.

"I'll start," Nova spoke faster the Janan could open her mouth. "There are some big, and I mean big, changes coming to the team, and we want you to be part of them."

"What she said," Janan added.

Shade softly sighed. "You both know I love the Bears, and I feel at home on the ice there, but so much has happened in my personal life. I don't think Manchester is the right place for me at this time." He tried to sound as professional as possible belting out his marriage was over.

"Have you been practicing that in a mirror?" Janan smarted off.

"Janan." Nova glared at her. "Leave him alone."

Instead of answering her cousin, she shook her head.

"Shade." Nova took over the conversation. "We're going to tell you something only a few know. We want you to keep it between us. Deal?"

He nodded. He would never betray their trust. They've been outstanding to him.

"Dad's retiring."

"What?" Shade's expression turned to shock. "Coach Long is retiring."

"Uncle Taden feels it's time for him to enjoy his life," Nova began to explain.

Taden Long, Janan's father and Nova's uncle, was the head coach for the New Hampshire Bears and had been for almost a decade. He was a beloved Bears' member.

"This means we need a coach," Nova continued.

Dubious to where this talk would be heading, he didn't say anything else and waited.

"You know we are getting closer to training camp, and it'll be harder for a new coach to come in and just "be ready"." Nova air quoted. "However, one is going to step up to the position."

"Who?" Shade racked his brain trying to think of who would step up to fill the shoes of Coach Long.

"Hamilton."

Of all the names in the world, of all the universe, Shade would have never ever thought the Bears' captain and Janan's husband, Hamilton Baer, would be the next coach.

"He's retiring as a player and going to take over this season and see how it goes." Nova kept talking as he tried to figure out what the hell was happening.

"Teo and Nathan will be traded."

This made him jump to his feet. "What? Both our goalies are going? Are you going to let Teo go?" His question was directed at Nova. She and Teo had been in a long-term relationship and had a child together.

"He's aware and understands this is for the good of the team," Nova disclosed to him. "I'm not happy, but this is about the Bears and not our personal life."

"Who's going to replace them? We can't start training camp with no goalies. Plus, someone is needed to take Hamilton's position." Even though he knew they were privy to this information, he felt the need to say it.

"We're in talks with Liam Green, Jacob Wallace, and Blake Naylor," Nova tried to reassure him.

She couldn't have said three bigger names in the PHL right now. Liam Green was the top goalie of the league. Jacob Wallace was number two and really not that far behind Liam. Then Blake Naylor was a complete powerhouse. Shade played against him for many, many years and lost more than won.

"Are you certain?" Shade wanted to be sure they were coming. All three of them would be the best contribution to the Bears.

"Over ninety percent sure," Janan jumped in.

"Wow." Shade sat back down and then reality hit. "Wait, why are you telling me this?"

"Because we want you to be the new captain," Nova said softly as if not to startle him.

"Wh…what? Me? Captain?" It was a word he never associated with himself.

"Shade, you're an essential piece to the Bears. The fans have loved you deeply. You're one of our top scorers and have been consistent since day one. The team respects you. You have the ability to keep everyone calm and focused even when Uncle Taden couldn't do it. You are a captain without the C. Now, this is your chance to have the official title." Nova's words were some of the kindest he'd heard in a long time.

"Have teams contacted you about me?" he inquired.

"You want the hard truth?" Janan questioned with a hard stare.

"Yes."

"Yes, they have, but I told them you were staying," she answered truthfully.

"Which was wrong," Nova jumped in. "I told her and Cabel."

Pushing his hand through his hair, he shouldn't have been shocked. Every time he called Cabel, he would say, "Nothing yet," and he knew he was lying.

"You belong in Manchester. You belong as a Bear. And you sure as hell belong as a captain," Janan stated.

He had no words. The reasons he needed to leave Manchester had nothing to do with the Bears. It had been because of his personal life. Sure, wearing the C on his chest was never a real dream but an honor all the same. He loved his teammates, staff, and everyone who worked with the Bears. Not to mention, a massive change in the coaching staff would rock the Bears and the PHL. A highly recognized player taking over the coaching slot would fill the headlines for weeks.

"You can think about it." Nova began to stand.

"Why?" Janan's voice cut in. "This is your chance to make a true difference in Bears' history."

"My marriage is over," he suddenly blurted out to them.

"Are you officially divorced?" she countered, not surprised by his statement.

"No."

"Then you have a chance to fix it. You can't do it if you're on the other side of the country playing for a different team. Plus, I don't take you as someone who runs away from a challenge."

The silence fell around them, and he let the conversation settle.

"Let me add this. Off the records, of course." Janan leaned closer to him. "If you stay as the captain, for one season and end up truly hating it, then I give you my word to trade you to the top team in the league. No matter how difficult it is. I promise you can leave."

He said nothing. They just stared at each other.

"We can give you until tomorrow to decide." Janan stood up.

"No." He sighed. "I know the answer already." He knew this change in his life would be a good one or the worst decision of his life.

CHAPTER SIX
Jenessa

When Jenessa received Greer's early morning text, she almost said no. Hot yoga at seven in the morning didn't sound pleasing. The only reason she went was because she loved yoga and had been enjoying Greer's company. Hot yoga never brought her joy. She didn't mind sweating…just not at *that* particular level.

"Morning." Greer's cheery greeting made her wonder how much caffeine she already had.

"Hey, Greer." Jenessa gave her a small smile, opened her mat and placed it near hers.

"I'm surprised you came. I figured you'd have to work."

"I do." She nodded. "But I don't have to be in right away."

In truth, she dreaded going into work today. She laid in bed for a while debating if she should take another sick day. Nothing seemed to motivate her to remove herself from the bed. Short of yoga.

The instructor strolled in as Jenessa felt the sweat began to form all over her body. No one smelled good or looked sexy after this class. Unless they were into the sweat/wet look. As the class began, Jenessa cleared her mind and started focusing on her poses. As she moved, she began to think about her life. Something she did with yoga. Shade, her job, Mikayla, her future. Mostly Shade.

Jenessa hadn't even been sleeping in their bed. She'd been falling asleep on the sectional in the den. Wrapping herself in his blanket gave her comfort and made her feel close to him. She hadn't said it out loud to anyone because she knew it sounded insane.

Continuing to follow the instructor, her job floated into the forefront. Tiffany had already sent her numerous texts regarding her schedule and reminding her not to forget the abundance of unread emails sitting in her inbox. None of which she read or answered back. She didn't care anymore. Her job had been a security blanket for her. Especially after Clay died. Work kept her pain away. Now, she's realizing it hadn't been the best way to deal with everything.

When the session ended, the instructor advised everyone to begin the meditation process. Jenessa sat in position and began to breathe in and out, clearing it all from her mind. Shade kept popping into her head, and she couldn't release the memories flooding her. The instructor told them to open their eyes and Jenessa felt the tears on her cheeks mixed in with all the sweat. Turning to Greer, she was given a small, sad smile. Any person would know the difference between sweat and tears. Jenessa wiped away the tears with a towel at the end of her mat and began gathering her items.

"Do you have time to get some juice?" Greer asked.

She knew by her tone, Greer hoped for her to say yes. Honestly, she couldn't say no. Having a drink with her would delay her going to work. "Sure."

After they ordered and received their drinks and found a table, Greer asked how she was doing.

"I'm taking everything day-by-day."

"You don't have to lie to me. How is it really going?"

She didn't know what happened or where it even came

from. However, the flood gates opened and Jenessa poured out her feelings. All of them.

"I told you Shade had come by and took some stuff and since that day, I have been more broken than ever before. It made it real. More real than him just leaving. He hadn't called me or contacted me in any way. Not to mention, I hate my job. I do. And I hate that Mikayla was right about it being a crutch. I have used work as an excuse for so long." She paused as the tears burned behind her eyes again. "I just want him and our life back."

"Then why aren't you contacting him?" Greer questioned. "Why are you waiting for him to call you?"

"Because for the past three years, he's been trying everything and anything to put our lives together and I've tried everything and anything to keep him at arm's length." She stared at her. "He's over it and me. He's given me a thousand chances to break out of my depression and pain—both of which I haven't yet—and he's done."

Greer slowly shook her head. "No, he's not. Edgar told him how sad he is."

Mikayla had told her the same thing, but she knew the little bit of pain he was feeling would go away once he moved on with his life. "He'll be better without me."

"You're wrong. You're one hundred percent wrong. You are going to regret not contacting Shade. He wants you as much as you want him. Both of you need to sit down and talk about it all. Get it out there in the open and fix it. It's the only way that you can truly heal."

Greer's words stuck with Jenessa as she left the studio and went back home to get ready for work. When she walked into the office, the words laid heavier on her heart. Heavy enough to cause her to forget about work. Three hours hadn't even passed, when she told Tiffany she was leaving and going home. Tiffany's shocked face said it all to her. She'd barely been to work since Shade left. Had it been a year ago, she would have gone even crazier leaving early. Today, she didn't care.

Jenessa drove around Manchester unsure where to go or what to do but had the whole day free to do whatever she wanted. There was one place she did love to go to. The library. Shade and she both loved to read and go to the library. She remembered on the weekends during the offseason, they would spend hours there. Reading and hanging out.

After she parked and was strolling up to the doors, she enjoyed the sun on her skin and face. Even though it was warm and humid, she welcomed it. She was free of the office. Inside the library, she began to head to the fictional section. Not looking for anything in particular, she just moved slowly up and down the aisles, glancing at the spines of books. Picking out a couple of books she headed over to one of the seating areas and relaxed on a couch then thumbed through the pages of the numerous books. She read several pages of each book, ensuring that they had captured her attention and then went to the checkout counter. Stopping at her favorite sub shop, she ordered her lunch to go and drove home.

When she walked into her home, she quickly dropped her items off in the den and raced upstairs. She stripped out of her clothes and slipped into a pair of sweats and one of Shade's T-shirts she'd hidden away. He didn't care she wore his clothes, but she still hid it. She washed off her makeup and twisted her hair into a messy top knot.

Once in the den, she laid out her sub on a small TV tray Shade had kept in there and then stretched her legs out onto the ottoman. Picking up her book, she let the quiet set in, and she embraced the world on the pages. She loved reading because it took her away from the real world around her. Many would believe she loved reading biographies. Many would never believe her go-to genre was romantic comedy. Long ago, she used to laugh all the time. She'd smile all the time. She was happy.

"Jenessa Wooten!"

Mikayla shouting from the front of the house made her jump and drop her book.

"What?"

"Why the hell aren't you answering your phone?" Her sister raced into the den, looking frantic.

"What's happened?" She leaped to her feet, panicked something was wrong with Shade.

"Look." Mikayla shoved her phone into her hand.

Jenessa's eyes had to focus on what she was looking at on the screen.

Shade Wooten possibly being traded to Idaho.

She read the words ten times. Her knees finally gave way, and she fell down onto the couch.

"He's gone."

"No." Mikayla bent down in front of her. "These are just rumors, but you can shut them down."

"How?" she asked breathlessly. Her heart was racing, and she couldn't breathe.

"Tell him. Tell him the truth. Tell him how much you love him. Tell him how much you want him back and what he means to you. Stop lying to yourself that you don't need him by your side." Mikayla had a single tear rolling down her cheek. "Don't let him leave without him knowing what your true feelings are for him."

Her words washed over her. Shade was getting ready to leave her and New Hampshire. She knew what he thought of this place. It was his home. He had told her so many times. Just like he told her she was his home.

"Are you even listening to me?" She took the phone from her hands.

Looking into her younger sister's eyes, she nodded.

"Go to him. He's at Jarvis's place right now."

Slowly, she shook her head. A lump formed in her throat cutting off her words

"You're a fool." Mikayla stood and without another word, she left Jenessa sitting on the sectional.

After the door slammed shut, Jenessa couldn't move from her spot. She reached for her phone and searched Shade's name. Numerous articles came up about his trade. He could go anywhere because he was so versatile as a player. Every season, he seemed to get better and better. She knew because she'd been watching him play since college. She hated it when she went to law school. Luckily, Shade had been drafted to Maine, and she was in Massachusetts.

Tossing her phone to the side, she slouched down into the cushions. The tears came, and she couldn't control them. Everything had finally hit her, and it made her think about their wedding day.

Jenessa had always wanted a big wedding and all the pomp and circumstance that came along with it. The big dress, the massive cake, all her family and friends with eyes on her. All of it.

Until Shade.

When she attended law school, it pained her to be away from him for a great length of time. But he was playing hockey, making a name for himself, and she was chasing her dream of being a lawyer. On the day she graduated from law school, Shade was traded to New Hampshire. After the graduation ceremony, Shade, Mikayla, her parents, and she all went out to celebrate at a fancy dinner.

Her parents never cared for Shade because he didn't come from money or a stable family background. But she didn't care about his past. The dinner had been a bit awkward until her parents called it a night and went back to their hotel. Shade, Mikayla, and Jenessa went to a local club. She wasn't a big partier, but she wanted to dance and drink the night away in Shade's arms.

A few drinks in, she watched Mikayla go off with some guy as she and Shade were grinding out on the dance floor. For the first time in a long time, she felt free. Free from school. Free from her parents. Free from it all. Even if it was for one night.

"When are you going to marry me?" she asked as they went back

to their table.

He sat down, and she chose to sit on his lap.

"Tomorrow," he answered without even thinking about it.

"You're just saying that because you want in my pants." She laughed.

"Nope. I will marry you first thing tomorrow. We'll wake up, shower, get married and then spend the day in my hotel room. Then we'll pack your apartment and go to Manchester and start our life."

This sobered her up quickly. "You're serious?"

"Yes," he said. "I love you and we're meant to be together forever."

Quickly, she pressed her lips to his and held him close. She wanted him right then and there, but somehow she controlled herself.

They continued to party throughout the night and when she woke up the next morning, she still remembered their conversation. Although, she didn't believe it would happen. They had never sat down and truly discussed their future. Albeit, they said to be together forever, and it was a struggle to make the long-distance relationship work, they never said the words until last night. In a club. Drinking.

"Good morning, Jen."

Rolling over, she saw Shade staring down at her. She realized he was freshly showered. "Why are you up? And dressed?"

"Because we have an appointment to get married today," he told her.

Before she could say anything, a loud knock on the door interrupted them.

"That's Mikayla." He informed her and headed to the door.

He barely had it opened before her sister burst through and jumped on the bed. "Wake up! Wake up! Someone is getting married today."

"What the hell, Kay?" She pushed her off the bed. "Are you both nuts?"

"No," they answered in unison.

"Come on and get up." Mikayla clapped her hands together in an effort to get her out of bed.

"We're not getting married," Jenessa clarified.

"Why not?" Shade's expression and tone of voice were full of

disappointment.

"Wait, you're serious?"

"Is there a reason you keep asking him that over and over?" *Mikayla interjected. "You should know by now if he said it, then he meant it."*

Shade nodded in agreement with her.

"So, get your ass up and let's go," Mikayla ordered.

"Give us a minute," she told her. "Go away and come back later."

Dramatically, Mikayla sighed and left the hotel room.

Shade came over and sat on the side of the bed. "Do you want to marry me?"

Jenessa fully sat up and cupped his face in her hands. "I want to marry you, but we're not spontaneous people. Are you sure you want to elope?"

"If you just want to be engaged and plan a huge wedding, then I will do it. However, I've wanted to marry you since I fell in love with you. I'll wait if I have to."

Happy tears filled her eyes, and she leaned in and kissed him. "I want to marry you...today."

"Then let me back in," Mikayla called from the other side of the door, causing them both to laugh.

Shade let her in, and she dragged Jenessa to the bathroom. Jenessa began to fumble over everything and got upset when she realized she didn't have anything white to wear. Mikayla managed to do her makeup and hair. Jenessa ended up wearing a red and white long maxi dress. Stepping out of the bathroom, Shade's mouth dropped.

"Beautiful as always." He wrapped his arms around her waist and kissed her.

"Stop making out and let's get married." Mikayla pushed them apart.

They used Jenessa's car to go to a wedding chapel that does quick ceremonies. Shade paid for it all. The two of them filled out the paperwork and waited for their turn.

"Are you nervous?" he asked, tightly holding her hand.

"Sort of wish my parents were here."

"Why?" Mikayla barked. "They don't even like Shade because he's not a descendant of some royalty or whatever."

Jenessa hated that Mikayla was right, but she was. Her parents wouldn't even acknowledge Shade half the time and definitely wouldn't approve of what was happening at this moment.

"Wooten?" the minister announced, and they all stood.

As the minister went through what was going to happen, Jenessa barely comprehended the words being said. All she knew was Shade and she would be married and together. At that moment, she didn't care about what dress she wore, or who was or wasn't there, only that Shade stood at the end of the aisle waiting for her.

The 'I do's' went perfectly. Their vows came from the heart. The kiss was perfection. She couldn't have planned it any better.

And   now   he   was   leaving.

CHAPTER SEVEN
Shade

Walking into the Bears' conference room, Shade's anxiety seemed to be shooting through the roof. It was the first day of training camp, and everyone's moods were the same. He took a seat near the front with Edgar on one side and Jarvis on the other. In front of him was Dag Limon who turned and grinned at him.

"Haven't seen you Woot? What's been going on?" Dag questioned.

"Not much," he lied. "How's Elexis?"

The name of his girlfriend caused him to smile broadly. "She's outstanding."

Not much more is said as Janan, Nova, Coach Long, and Cabel went up to the front. Everyone in the room quieted down and waited to hear what was about to be said.

"I'd like to welcome you all to training camp," Nova began. "We all feel this season is going to be the best yet. However, it will be starting off with some changes."

His leg began to bounce up and down. Shade couldn't stop the nervous tick. He had no memory of ever being this crazed. Not even on his wedding day. Thinking of Jenessa made his eyes close, and he took a slow deep breath.

"Uncle Tad." Nova turned toward Coach Long.

Taden Long rubbed his bearded chin as he took a step forward. Shade glanced around the room, checking out everyone's expressions. They were all confused as to why Coach stood up there. He watched Coach compose himself before speaking.

"I have been a Bear for over a decade. I consider Manchester home. However, things have happened in my life." He paused slightly hanging his head, unable to go on.

The entire PHL world knew of Coach Long's past. Hell, the entire world knew. The room felt his pain but said nothing as they waited for him to continue.

"No one has ever had an easy life," he spoke again. "I've never had the luxury of knowing what freedom is without strings attached. I don't mean I'm chained to the PHL or my contract but with life in general. This offseason, I took time for me. Something I've never ever done. I'm always putting others first, and I don't mind it. However, I needed to do something for me. Something to bring me happiness. As much as hockey has brought me joy, it was also a distraction of my reality. But not anymore."

Everyone watched intently as his eyes welled up.

"I'm retiring."

The statement made everyone gasp. All but Shade. He knew the words were coming, but they still pained him. Coach Long would be in the PHL Hall of Fame as a player and a coach. He still had a lot of good years in front of him and there could always be the possibility of him returning.

"I'm very lucky to have had the career that I have had, but my heart isn't in it the way it should be. You all deserve a coach whose full attention is on the game."

As Taden finished, Cabel began clapping. The room stood, giving him the true sendoff he deserved. After he left Nova brought the attention to her again.

"I know you all are worried because today is the first day of training camp and you think we don't have a coach. You see, Dad told us a while ago about his intentions for this season. Janan, Cabel, and I have been searching for someone to come in and take over. However, we couldn't really find anyone we felt "fit"." She air quoted the last word.

"Then someone came in and sat down to option for the job." Cabel took over. "We were all uncertain about this person because he's a player and never coached before. He sat with us, laid out a plan for the team, and impressed us all."

Shade felt a shift in the room as many of the guys leaned forward or moved in their seats.

"He's going to retire from his position and the team to become our coach," Nova said.

A dramatic pause caused everyone to hold their breath. Then Hamilton Baer, stood and moved to the front of the room. All the players began to cheer, hoot, and carry on as he just stood at the head of the room. Shade caught Janan and Hamilton gazing at each other, and it made him think of Jenessa all over again. They used to look at each other as if no one else but they were in the room.

Once the guys quieted down, Hamilton addressed them. "I know this is a massive change. Yes, I'm retiring. Nonetheless, I believe in you all, and I hope you have the same faith in me. I know we will have an amazing season."

The room erupted in applause for him. Shade had been playing with him for a long time and knew he would be an outstanding coach. He loved hockey and everything that went with it. Hamilton would give his blood, sweat, and limbs to the Bears, no matter what title he held.

"Settle down." Janan raised her voice, and the group quieted. "We have a couple more things to discuss. First, you've not heard but we've traded Nathan and Teo."

This made the guys look around. Shade caught a glimpse of Alden Brockman. Nathan dated his sister and was the father of her baby. He seemed sad. They all knew Alden and Nathan were close friends.

"Yes, we did, but we've obtained Liam Green and Jacob Wallace, who will be here tomorrow. And we're in talks for someone else to replace Hamilton's spot."

Everyone let the names of their new goalies sink in. The room seemed extremely pleased to have two of the biggest goalies in the league on their team.

"Who's our new captain?" Ladd asked from the back of the room.

"First, we wanted someone who would help you *boys* stay in line." Janan glared at them all. "This position is more than a C on a uniform. Even though there are several guys who would be proud to wear it, we have one who will help lead us to the championship." Again, another dramatic pause. "We picked Shade."

His ears began to ring as the room cheered for him. Jarvis and Edgar began tugging and grabbing at him, making him stand up. Nova waved him up toward her, and he slowly made his way up front.

"I know we all heard the rumors about him being traded, but this morning he signed a contract to stay," Janan explained, leaving the part out that it was only for one year.

He was uncertain if this decision would cause him more heartache. Being in Manchester only brought up memories of Jenessa. He couldn't even eat out without something reminding him of her. However, he had loyalty to this team and right now, they needed him more than Jenessa wanted him.

"All right," Janan yelled out to the room. "Let's get some physicals done."

The guys began shuffling out of the room when Shade felt a hand on his shoulder.

"This is going to be a crazy ride."

Shade nodded at Hamilton's remark. "Yes. Let's hope we survive it. The media is going to tear us apart and nitpick everything we do."

He agreed. "I guess we need to give them something to talk about." He slapped Shade on the back as he walked ahead of him.

As the team went through their rigorous physicals, the guys kept coming up to Shade to offer him congratulations about wearing the big C.

"Mikayla's going to shit when she hears you're staying," Jarvis said, wiping the sweat from his brow with the bottom of his T-shirt. "Why didn't you say anything to us?"

"Janan and Nova told me not to," he said truthfully.

"Are you happy?" Edgar asked when he walked up to them.

"Yes, because I love being a Bear…" He paused, not finishing his thought.

"Then why aren't you happier?" Edgar called him out.

"I can't celebrate with my wife," he confessed.

"Have you talked to her?"

"No."

"Then how do you know you can't celebrate with her?" he countered.

Before he could tell him he didn't think she would want to see him, his name was called to the next station. He tried his best not to think about Edgar's question and put his focus on the instructions being given to him. When he finished he went to the water station. As he took several gulps, Jackson came up to him.

"Hey, Captain." He smirked.

"Guess I'll have to get used to that."

"It fits you. I think you'll be an outstanding captain."

Even though many still had a bad taste in their mouths about Jackson, Shade saw he was trying to change.

"Thanks, Jackson." He knew by the tone he meant it to be genuine. "Are you ready?"

The simple question had a lot of meaning behind it, not needing to be explained out loud.

"Yes, I'm going to show the haters what I'm able to do." Determination filled Jackson's eyes.

"I can't wait." He gave him a slap on the back as he moved through the gym.

Everyone began to finish up as the team moved toward the cafeteria. The team lunch would give the officials time to get the results of the physicals. Shade filled up his plate with the delicious food and took a seat at one of the emptier tables. It didn't take long before there were guys surrounding him.

The conversation quickly moved to all the changes. Albeit, it was a crazy meeting, everyone expressed their excitement about Hamilton as the coach and Liam and Jacob coming to the team. Shade felt the same way. He did hate to see Nathan and Teo leave but understood the reasoning for it. They were great guys, but their numbers were lacking this past season. The topic about other PHL teams brought their discussion full circle as they finished eating.

Cabel told everyone to return to the conference room. Once the group settled into their seats, he announced that everyone passed their physicals. He then turned the floor over to Hamilton. Shade wasn't surprised when the lights dimmed and the projector turned on. He knew their new coach would be prepared. The guys focused on the plays he began to run through.

He'd grown used to Hamilton's serious demeanor, but this was a new level. He stood taller. His voice stronger and determination oozed off him. Shade studied the plays and was impressed by what he showed. Hamilton had been around long enough, and he knew the game. Anyone looking in from the outside would think he'd been a coach for years.

A couple of hours passed before Hamilton dismissed them to go to the media room. He told them all to be suited up for tomorrow's practice. Shade mentally prepared himself because he knew they would be wanting to talk to him.

"Damn, this season is going to be off the chain," Zerrick said next to Shade and Jarvis.

"Did you use the term *off the chain*?" Jarvis had to stop walking to ask his question.

"Yes. How else would you say it?" Zerrick asked.

"Something besides *off the chain*," Jarvis mumbled and started walking again.

Shade chuckled at the two of them. Just before they were about to reach the media room, his name was called out from behind him.

"Hi, Kian," he greeted the PR director.

"Congratulations on the new title." Kian Wick grinned.

"Thanks." He would need to stop feeling weird when people commented on his new position.

"I want you to meet Cat." Kian turned slightly to the young female standing behind him. "She's our new PR assistant."

The blonde with big blue eyes held out her hand. "Pleasure to meet you."

"Same." Shade gave her hand a simple, firm shake and released it.

"She's going to help you navigate your interviews this afternoon," Kian explained.

"Okay." He nodded. "Lead the way." He gave her a small smile. He thought he noticed her cheeks flush but ignored it.

"You're going to be bombarded today with questions about your trade rumors and becoming captain," Cat stated as they walked. "It would be best to keep your answers short and sweet."

He listened as she continued to talk about what he should and shouldn't say.

"You act as if you've been doing this for a while," he commented as they reached the door of the media room.

"I worked for the Tigers for the past three years," she told him.

"You look like you're barely out of high school."

Cat giggled and touched his arm. "I'm twenty-six. I just look young."

She gave his arm a slight squeeze and bit her bottom lip. Dropping her hand, she opened the door for him. Inside the small room, the reporters began asking questions all at once. It took him a second to get his bearings.

The voices seemed to be rapid firing at him. Normally, Shade would be perfectly fine with the media, but he never had this many coming at him all at once. When he completed his media session, Cat escorted him to what the players would call the 'photograph room'.

Here he was given his new jersey with a bright C on its chest. He hadn't been too emotional about being captain until that moment. He wished Jenessa was here with him because they would always do a family photo. Again, Edgar's words came back to haunt him. As he tried to remain focused Jenessa continued to float in his thoughts.

Finally, he managed to get away from everyone and out to his car before anyone could grab at him again. He wanted to call Jenessa. There was nothing else he wanted to do but tell her about his day. Staring at her name on his cell phone screen, he wanted to tap it, but he stopped himself. By now, someone at her office would have told her about him staying in New Hampshire, yet she still hasn't reached out to him.

Setting the phone down, he started his truck and made his way to Jarvis's condo.

Opening the door, Shade realized he'd need to find his own place and soon. Especially since he'll be here for another season. He figured he'd lease a small apartment, nothing overly expensive.

"Jarvis?"

"It's me, Joy," Shade answered Jarvis's younger sister.

She came into the kitchen where he was grabbing something to drink. "Hey, Shade. Or should I say Captain?" she joked.

He gave her a smile. "Shade is fine."

"The Bears have been the talk of the day and not just on sports sites," she informed him.

"Janan and Nova like to make it big." He chuckled. "How are you doing?"

She shrugged. "The defense asked for another continuance."

"Why?" Shade's disbelief had to be known. Joy's rapist, a serial rapist, had been in jail for the past few months.

"They gave some lame reason about needing more time to prepare." She appeared as if she may cry.

"Is he still in jail?"

The asshole was the governor's son and they all worried he'd receive bail. Thankfully, the judge refused any bail and kept him in jail.

"Yes, for now."

"I know you're tired of hearing people say not to worry, but he is still in jail."

Again, she nodded. "True."

Deciding to change the topic he asked how she liked being Jarvis's assistant.

"It's not too bad." She gave him an actual smile. "However, the DMs are filled with females throwing themselves at him. Even though he's with Mikayla and everyone knows it."

"Yeah, that's why I don't answer or look at any of my DMs." He made the mistake many years ago and quickly learned to never ever do it again. Then again, he doesn't do much social media posting. Some of the guys couldn't stay away from it, others never touch it.

"I guess since you're staying here, the homelife is still on the rocks."

"Yes."

"Have you talked to her?"

This question seemed to be the most asked of him. Right behind 'how are you doing?'.

"No."

"Are you going to?"

Normally, he wouldn't answer but something inside him told him to.

"I want to. I just don't think she wants to hear from me."

"Why do you think that?"

"Because for the past three years, I've done everything I can think of to get us to some sort of normalcy, but nothing has worked."

Joy took in his words before saying, "Then I wouldn't call her."

This made him freeze. Everyone had been telling him to call and talk to her. Joy had been the first not to say it.

"Seriously," she continued. "You're one of the nicest guys on this planet. Most husbands wouldn't have stayed as long as you did. But you love her. If she can't see everything you've done or are doing to make your marriage work, then you need to leave. It'll be hard and painful, but life is too short not to be happy. And if anyone deserves happiness, it's you."

Shade leaned against the counter, letting everything sink in. Her words made sense; even he knew it. He thought back to all the things he tried to do for his marriage and Jenessa. All the love he showed her with nothing in return. All the pain he endured without a shoulder to lean on when he needed it. He went through his heartache alone. When he and Jenessa committed themselves to each other, he thought they would go through their trials and tribulations together.

But he was alone.

"Thanks, Joy."

He pushed himself off the counter and went into the

bedroom. As he shut the door, he pulled out his cell phone. He had saved a number in his contacts and hoped he would never use it. Today, he knew the inevitable was happening.

Waiting for the woman on the other end of the phone to finish the greeting, he said, "My name is Shade Wooten, and I need a divorce attorney."

CHAPTER EIGHT
Jenessa

At six-thirty a.m., Jenessa's ears were ringing as her boss expressed his disappointment with her since she was taking yet another day off from work. She knew there were a million and one things to do in the office, but she brushed it off anyway and didn't care about the consequences because today would be different…she had plans. She had made the choice to have a day for herself. She used to do this years ago but having a job kept her busier than she ever imagined. Never having time for herself. Instead of arguing with him, she simply listened and then hung up when he finished.

Then she went back to sleep.

For the first time—probably in her entire life—Jenessa slept in. Almost to noon. There had been no real explanation as to why she slept so late, but once her eyes were open, she felt rested. She hadn't felt that way in years.

First on her list: a run.

As her feet rhythmically hit the pavement on the park trail, she thought about Shade. Jenessa really never was a runner, but Shade had gotten her into the activity. Now, she loved it. But like yoga, she never had time.

Her stride hit about the second mile as did memories

of Shade. When she followed him to Manchester, she didn't have a large paycheck coming in. Even though they were married, she wanted to contribute to the finances as much as possible. It didn't take long for her to figure out they were a team, and it didn't matter who made what. He never made her feel as if he were better than her because he made more. She remembered house hunting with him. He hadn't had a real budget in mind, but Jenessa had a steno pad of wants and a budget lined out for each option. Shade never commented on anything and just let her do her thing.

When she finished her run and went back home, she really looked at the place. It was a beautiful house, with four bedrooms, two and a half bathrooms, and every room larger than the next. But without Shade in it with her, it wasn't home. Just a place to live.

Strolling up the stairs to the bedroom, she ran her hand along the varnished wood, wondering if Shade cared about the finishing of the wood as much as she did. Already knowing the answer to be no, she went into the bedroom and opened her side of the closet. Designer outfits, shoes, and purses for every event, occasion, or just everyday attire stared back at her.

Opening Shade's side, she knew it would be empty but remembered everything in it. Five suits, none of which were high-end designer suits. Three would be black, one gray, and one navy blue. Five crisp white dress shirts and eight ties. His everyday clothing consisted of three pairs of jeans and less than ten shirts. His shoes were a couple of pairs of gym shoes, a pair of loafers and one pair of dress shoes. She would always buy him clothes but learned early on, it was a waste because he wouldn't wear fancy named clothing. It made him uncomfortable so she stopped doing it. She wondered if after nine years, did she really know him. Pushing the thought away, she grabbed some clean clothes and jumped in the shower.

The warm shower calmed her muscles and cleaned

away the sweat and grime from running outside. She let her towel-dried hair hang as she slipped into a pair of skinny jeans and a T-shirt. She left her face natural only putting on a swipe of nude gloss.

Stepping out of the bedroom, she stopped and glanced down the hallway. She avoided looking down there more than anything. Where happy memories should be, only held pain. She hadn't been in that *room* since the day before she went to the hospital. Everything felt fine. Nothing was wrong.

Then it all went to hell.

Grabbing her keys and purse, she knew exactly where to go to hide away. Even if only for a few hours.

Jenessa pushed the button to ensure every kernel had butter on it. Picking up the massive container of popcorn, she managed to get in the correct theater. Settling in her seat, she glanced around, seeing hardly anyone there. Then again, it was the afternoon on a work day.

The lights dimmed as the bright screen illuminated the theater. Jenessa focused on nothing but her popcorn and the romantic comedy in front of her. The outside world and the pain she had didn't exist. Nothing beyond those movie theater doors were important to her.

Until the end credits rolled and the lights grew brighter then she had to face it again.

As she drove home, she remembered all the times her stress levels were extremely high, and she'd hide in a movie theater. Especially if the library wasn't open. Like books, movies helped her relax and shut the world away. Any other time, she'd have a little more perspective when she walked out. Now, she felt the same as when she entered.

Not paying attention to which way she headed home, she ended up in traffic around the arena. Jenessa's eyes scanned the large crowd of fans crossing the street decked out in Bears' gear. Banners hung from the lamp posts and on buildings. One caught her attention:

New Coach. New Captain. New Season.

Blinking hard to fight the tears, it had been over three weeks since the announcement was made about Shade's new contract and captain status. Desperately she wanted to call and congratulate him but always stopped herself. He didn't want to hear from her. His life was moving on and without her in it. Hell, apparently for the better. He didn't need—or want—her to be bothering him. Elation had filled her as she heard the news on the radio while driving home from work. She almost had to pull over as the tears fell from her eyes. He deserved it.

Once she managed her way through the traffic and made it home, she turned on the TV in the den. The Bears' opener came onto the screen in front of her. Jenessa had stopped going to games after Clay passed away. She tried to go to some events but feared seeing Nova and her baby. Even though Nova had to be the nicest person in the world, she couldn't bear to see the beautiful little girl because the reminder was too hard.

Since she wouldn't go to the arena, Jenessa watched the games on TV. She never told Shade she saw the games because…well, she didn't know why she never said anything. Nonetheless, she stretched out on the sectional, intently watching the Bears' warm-ups. The sports reporters were saying how outstanding the Bears were going to be this season. The camera panned to the goalie, Liam. Last year, he sat at the top of the PHL ratings, has played in several championship games, and was an overall powerhouse in the net.

The camera found Janan and Nova in the owner's box. The discussion carried on for a few moments evaluating the changes and what were they thinking. Cabel came into the frame and the conversation moved to him and what their takes were on the topic. Jenessa understood the change and thought overall it was good for the Bears. She really enjoyed the part where Shade stayed.

On cue, her husband's face came onto the screen, causing her heart to race. His stunning brown eyes were bright even through the TV. Sitting a bit forward she hung on his every word.

"Shade, how are you enjoying being a captain?" the reporter asked.

"I'm very honored to be named captain to one of the greatest teams in the PHL," he answered confidently.

"How is the team dealing with the changes?" the reporter continued.

"We all figured there was going to be an adjustment, but now that Blake Naylor is here, the team has really come together." Again, Shade's strong voice gave the assurance the Bears were going all the way this season.

"Thanks, Shade. I'm sure your family will be cheering loud for you tonight."

Jenessa saw the pain wash over his face.

"Thanks," had been the only word he said before skating off.

She knew Mikayla and the fans would cheer for Shade, but he didn't have any true family. When he had told her about his past it almost broke her. They hadn't been dating long before Jenessa wanted to have him meet her family. At the time, she and Mikayla were practically inseparable. When she first introduced him to her, they became instant best friends. And they've been that way ever since.

When the time came to meet her parents, she had warned him about how he could possibly be treated. To this point, she never really asked about his family life because he would simply say he had no family and changed the topic. She assumed there had been a rift in his homelife dynamics. She never imagined how it truly had been.

Her parents had chosen to take them to "The Club". Jenessa and Mikayla hated going to the country club. Her sister expressed it more than Jenessa but agreed with the rants. She tried to convince her parents to go somewhere else, but she lost the argument.

However, Shade didn't seem phased by "The Club" one bit. Not even with his ill-fitting suit. He walked in, self-assured of himself, holding her hand. She saw her parents' expression of disdain as they laid eyes on him. A surge of protection washed over Jenessa. She didn't want her parents to hurt his feelings.

Shade stood proudly next to her as she introduced him to her parents. He extended his hand, and she studied her parents as they reluctantly returned the handshake. He pulled out Jenessa's chair for her to sit down, and he seemed to not even blink at all the judgmental glares on him.

After they ordered their drinks, an awkward silence fell over the table. Mikayla had been the one to start talking to Shade about hockey. This seemed to please him, and he began talking to her. Again, Jenessa saw the disgust on her parents' faces.

"What kind of name is Shade?" Her mother's lip curled as if his name left a bad taste in her mouth.

He shrugged. "It's the one on the birth certificate."

"How did your parents come up with it?" she asked.

"I'm not sure."

"Did you not question your mother about it?" her mother continued.

"Not that I recall," he answered. "How did you create such beautiful names for your daughters?" He turned it around on them.

"We wanted something memorable. So men would remember them." Her father finally spoke.

"And we're pretty enough to be offered two goats and two cows," Mikayla joked sarcastically about their non-existent dowry.

Shade and Jenessa both had to cover up their laughter when her parents shot daggers across the table.

The waitress came by and took their order. When she left, her father continued the questioning.

"Are you from Buffalo?"

"Yes, born and raised."

"And what does your family do?"

Jenessa grew angry by the question. Not to mention embarrassed as well. Nothing bothered her more than her parents need to be at the top of some invisible social circle.

"I don't have any family," Shade answered.

This made her mother laugh. "Boy, you must have a family."

Another personality trait Jenessa truly disliked about her parents. They used the words boy or girl when addressing those they think were below them.

Shade glanced at Jenessa, and she saw the pain in his eyes before facing her parents.

"I have no family," he repeated.

"I don't understand why you can't answer a simple question, boy." Her father's tone grew firm.

Jenessa opened her mouth to give her father a piece of her mind, but Shade started to speak before she could.

"Well, all right, man. I don't know who my father is because my mother had been a prostitute since she was a teenager. Somehow—and no one knows how—I managed to make it to eight years old before my crack-addicted mother walked out one day. I almost starved to death before I finally left the apartment to find food in a dumpster. It was there the police found me and put me in the foster system until I was kicked out at eighteen. Luckily, I graduated high school early so I managed to start college shortly thereafter. Now, here I am...in a very swanky country club."

Everyone's jaws were dropped. She thought her mother might faint. Jenessa went to reach for him, but he stood up.

"Thanks for dinner." He tossed the expensive cloth napkin down and rushed away from the table.

"Jenessa, you're never to see that boy again," her father seethed.

She pushed her chair back and got up. "Dad, I'm going to marry him." She never knew why she said those words or where they even came from, but she meant every...single...syllable.

"If you don't I will," Mikayla added.

Not waiting to hear another word from her parents, she ran away from the table. She had to tell Shade everything that was weighing on her mind.

"Shade! Shade!" Her heels were killing her feet as she ran as fast as she could to catch up to him.

He stopped and turned to her without saying anything.

"Please..." She tried to catch her breath. "Please don't think

I'm like them."

"Jen, I will never have that." He pointed to the country club. "I'm not from somewhere fancy, and I'll probably never have anything fancy."

"I don't care. None of it matters to me. Only you. Only you matter to me. I love you."

"I like you too."

They both turned to see Mikayla standing a bit behind them, holding Jenessa's purse.

"I like you too, Kay." Shade grinned. His focus returned to Jenessa. "And I love you." He cupped her face and pressed his lips to hers.

"Okay, let's die down the PDA, people," Mikayla groaned at their public display of affection.

This made them both laugh against their lips. They pulled apart but were still holding onto each other.

"I'm hungry. Let's get some burgers," Mikayla suggested then headed toward Jenessa's car.

"I'm sorry about tonight," Jenessa said softly when she thought her sister was out of earshot. "And I'm sorry about your childhood."

"You don't have to apologize for anything." Shade held her. "Just know I'll always love you."

"Me too."

Jenessa wiped a stray tear away as she focused on the TV. The score had been tied one to one, and she couldn't figure out where the time had gone because the third period was almost over.

Watching the screen, she caught a glimpse of Shade jumping the boards. She could pick him out from anywhere on the ice. The camera was panned out, and her eyes never left him. Jarvis passed the puck to him, and he quickly moved it to Zerrick. He settled it down before chucking it back to Shade. Jenessa held her breath as Shade raised his stick, pulling it back and slapping the puck with perfect precision. As if it was planned, it sailed passed the goalie and hit the back of the net.

She clapped and even yelled out a *woo-hoo* as the camera

zoomed in on him celebrating with his teammates. Her heart fell because Shade wasn't smiling. He looked...heartbroken.

This made her drop her gaze from his face. He always smiled and joked around with his team and friends. Now, a deadness stained his eyes and face. She couldn't handle it and turned off the TV. Moving through the house, there wasn't anything to do or anyone to talk to.

Reaching the top of the stairs, her eyes went to the *door*. Her legs carried her past the master bedroom and stopped in front of it. She couldn't go in. Her hand wouldn't even touch the handle. Instead, she pressed her back against the hallway wall and slid down. Her brain rushed memories to her forefront.

The first was when she found out she was pregnant. Shade and she had discussed what would happen if she did become pregnant.

Shade had been out of town when she thought she had gotten a flu bug. She continued to work, but she couldn't keep anything down. Every time she ate, it came right back up.

Pregnancy hadn't even crossed her mind until Mikayla brought it up. Jenessa rushed to the drugstore and bought several boxes of pregnancy tests. As much as she wanted to take them at that moment, she had to wait. She knew the morning time would be the best. Plus, she wanted Shade to be there.

Somehow she managed to sleep through the night and was just starting to wake up when she heard Shade coming in the door. She sat up the moment he strolled into the bedroom.

"I didn't mean to wake you, baby. I took the red-eye flight so I could get home to you quicker." He set his bag down and gave her a quick kiss.

"You didn't wake me. We need to talk." She held tight to his hand and made him sit next to her on the bed.

"Baby, what's wrong?" Concern and confusion filled his voice and face.

"I think I might be pregnant," she said it matter of fact.

Shade's face paled for just a second before a gigantic smile appeared. "Yes," he yelled, jumping off the bed.

His excitement made her sit back. She knew he'd be happy but did not expect this reaction.

"Shade. Shade." She had to get him to focus again. "I've not taken the test yet. I don't know if I am. I wanted you to be here when I found out."

"Take it. Take it now! Do you have to pee? I can get you some water." His words came out fast, and she could barely understand him.

She grabbed his wrist as he tried to bolt toward the door to get her some water. "Stop. Calm yourself." She forced him to sit down. "I have to pee. I don't need water. However, I need you to calm down because I'm freaking out here."

As if she flipped on a light switch, Shade relaxed and cupped her face.

"I'm here. This is going to be great. Whatever you need or want I will get." He kissed her softly.

"I'm going to pee and then we'll figure out what to do after we get the results." She tried to sound confident, but her mind raced, and her insides flipped.

"I'll go with you." Shade began to make his way to the bathroom.

"Shade Wooten!" She gasped. "I can pee. Alone!"

"I know. I know." He stepped back. "I just don't know what to do."

She felt bad for snapping at him. Gently she tugged on his wrist and guided him over to the bed and sat down with him.

"Stay here and wait for me. I'll only be a minute." She kissed his cheek and went into the bathroom, closing the door.

When she finished and came out, Shade had remained on the bed. His legs bounced up and down. Over the years, she knew he had that nervous tick when he was the most anxious. Kneeling down in front of him, she placed her hands on his knees to help make the jerking stop.

"Talk to me," she said softly.

"What if I'm a bad father?" he whispered.

"If I know anything in this world, it's there isn't a bad bone in

your body. You'll be an amazing father because you're an amazing person."

Every word she spoke was the absolute truth. Shade oozed kindness and love. It would only multiply with their child. She moved up to kiss his lips. The kiss deepened and Shade pulled her into his lap. They continued to share their passion for several minutes. Jenessa always loved the way he kissed. A perfect mix of firm to get his point across that he wanted her but soft to show his tenderness.

"You know how to calm me down," he stated with a smile when they broke apart for air.

"Because I love you."

"I love you."

They briefly kissed before she said, "Are you ready to look?"

"Yes, and no matter what I love you," Shade said.

"Me too."

*He helped her to her feet, and they held hands as they walked into the bathroom. On the sink counter was a small white stick with a blue cap. They looked at the display—*Pregnant.

Shade grabbed her face and kissed her. Then he picked her up in his strong arms. Over and over again he said how much he loved her. She could feel it.

She never felt more love.

"Nes!"

Mikayla's voice brought her back to reality.

"Here," she said barely audible, remaining on the hallway floor.

Her sister came up the stairs and slowed when she saw Jenessa on the floor. Not saying anything, she immediately sat next to her, looping her arm through Jenessa's. Mikayla rested her head on Jenessa's shoulder.

"You smell like nacho cheese," Jenessa said, making them both giggle.

"I ate at the game," she informed her.

"I watched it."

"I knew you would," Mikayla stated.

"He did good."

"He did," Mikayla agreed.

They sat quietly as the tears flowed softly. She thought of Shade, her baby, all the pain inside her. Shade needed to be happy and all she had done to him during the past three years was cause him heartache. He had tried time and time again to bring her out of the world of darkness she'd taken up residence in and every time she'd push him away, by being rude, yelling at him, or just ignoring him altogether.

For three years, she treated him like…nothing.

It's definitely not something one would do to the love of their life. No person that you claim to love, especially someone you love as much as she loved Shade, should be treated the way she treated him. To her, during those times, he was just some guy living with her. A roommate.

"I brought you something." Mikayla sat up and reached for the bag next to her. Jenessa didn't even notice it. She placed it on her lap.

Opening it, the first thing she saw was a dark brown jersey. Then bright golden letters which spelled out Wooten." Pulling it out, she saw the number fifty-seven. Turning it around the big C was shining. She ran her fingertips around it, touching the thick material and stitching.

"Call him."

Jenessa said nothing and continued to stare at the jersey.

"He stayed, Nes. This is your chance for you to tell him the truth. To tell him how sorry you are and how much you love him." Mikayla's gentle tone made her tears fall faster.

"I can't do it," Jenessa finally said.

"Why?" she pushed.

"Because he's better without me."

"No…he's not." She gritted her teeth. "You're being a fool. If you keep this up you'll lose him forever."

With her words, she knew losing him would kill her soul and spirit, but he'd be happy. She'd hurt him for so long, he deserved to be happy.

Without her.

CHAPTER NINE
Shade

Focusing on the stick handling drill, Shade tried to clear his mind the best he could. But today would be harder than most. His stick moved the puck with his commands but stopped when someone slapped his shoulder.

Turning, he saw Hamilton slightly glaring at him.

"Practice is over."

Shade nodded.

"Are you okay?"

He nodded again.

"You seem a lil lost today."

Shade caught wind of the southern accent Hamilton normally hid well. "Just a lot on my mind."

"Anything you need help with?"

"Nah, I'm good." He skated off the ice and strolled to the visitor locker room.

The Bears were on a road game in his hometown of Buffalo. Being here, especially since today was his birthday, had always carried a bittersweet feeling. He loved the city because this was where he met Jenessa. It carried many memories of happiness. He'd pushed away the bad ones and only focused on the good. The ones with them together and him playing hockey.

When he finished changing out of his gear and showered, he joined the team on the bus to go back to the hotel. Edgar sat next to him on the ride.

"She call you yet?"

Shade shook his head, knowing he was asking about Jenessa.

"Have you talked to her?"

Saying nothing, he turned his attention out the window, staring at the city passing him by. Thankfully, the trip had been short, and Edgar stopped bothering him with any further questions.

Once in the hotel, he dropped off his items in his room and headed out. He ordered an Uber to pick him up and take him directly to a rent a car station. In no time, he had his own vehicle and was driving. At first, he didn't know where to go. He only knew he didn't want to be at the hotel. He had several hours before the bus would be leaving for the game. He had time to explore memory lane.

Driving toward the least popular part of the city, Shade's memory of the street hadn't changed much. Pulling into a spot across a run-down brick building, he noticed several drug dealers and numerous ladies strolling the sidewalks looking for "dates".

The memory of the day his mother left racked his mind. It seemed liked yesterday.

His mother sat on the ratty, broken down couch. Her long brown hair looked like she hadn't washed or combed it in a month. She kept jerking and fidgeting and had sores on her skin.

"Mom, I'm hungry," Shade's tiny voice said.

She grunted something, but he didn't know what she said. He remained on the small chair in the corner where he could watch the street below. His stomach hurt as he stared at his mom.

"I'm leaving." She managed to stand and left the apartment.

Shade turned to look out the window. A moment later he saw her on the sidewalk. She started going left for several steps before heading to the right then across the street. His eyes never left her until she was completely out of view.

Sitting there, the world continued to move about in front of him. As the sun set, the sidewalks filled with more people. He finally moved away from the view and went to the kitchen. He climbed up to the counter and opened the cupboards—empty. He didn't have to look in the fridge. Food hadn't been in there for months. He did get a drink of water from the tap and went back to the chair. Resting his arms on the ledge, he closed his eyes and listened to the outside world.

Shade felt the heat from the sun on his face. He had remained on the ledge all night. As usual. Leaning back the pain in his stomach grew worse, his mouth felt like sand, and he was weak.

Wandering around the tiny apartment he hoped he could find something to eat. As if the universe heard his wish, he found a small jar of peanut butter in the back of the hall closet. Instantly, he knew she had hidden it for herself.

Managing to get the lid off, he dug his fingers into the jar and then shoved the contents into his mouth. The sweetness hitting his taste buds made him moan. He ate several scoops with his fingers before placing the jar back into the closet. He drank another cup of tap water and returned to his chair.

This continued for almost three whole days. Shade worried. Not about his mother. He was eight years old. Definitely old enough to know she was never coming back. It surprised him she stayed as long as she had. Staring down at the now-empty peanut butter jar, he wasn't sure what to do next.

Another twenty-four hours passed, and the hunger pains came back. Deep down, Shade knew he had to go find some food. He slipped his dirty feet into his only pair of shoes he owned. They had holes in the soles, but he never complained. He shut the door and walked down several flights of stairs, passing a lot of trash, drug paraphernalia, one guy passed out, and rats.

Outside, he started toward the right. He knew people would come this way with pizza boxes. No one seemed to pay any attention to him as he continued down the sidewalk. About two blocks up, a pizza parlor sat on the corner. The aroma made Shade's stomach growl. He had pizza a few times in his life and remembered he enjoyed it. However, he knew he couldn't just walk in and sit down. Instead, he went into the alley. A massive blue dumpster sat near the door marked Pappy's Pizza.

Letting his instincts take over he stood on his tiptoes, trying to peek over the edge. He couldn't see anything and wasn't strong enough to pull himself up. There were crates next to the dumpster. Dragging one over, he stepped on it, finally able to peer in. On top of a large black garbage bag was a discarded pizza box.

Flipping it open, there was already eaten crust, but there were two uneaten slices of pizza. Shade's mouth watered, and his stomach growled even more. Everything in him screamed for him to eat it. Picking up one slice, he took a bite of the rock-hard pizza. He didn't care as he took bite after bite until reaching the crust. Then he grabbed the other slice and did the same.

As he was about to take his last bite, he heard a car pulling up near him. Glancing over his shoulder, he watched two large police officers stepping out of their car.

"Hey, son," the one who was on the passenger side greeted him.

Shade didn't answer but did take the last bite of the pizza in his hand.

"Where's your mom?"

Staying quiet, he remembered all the times he watched the police outside the window. Some were really mean. These two didn't seem to be that way.

"Where's your dad?"

The same officer continued to question, but Shade kept his mouth shut after swallowing the mouthful.

"Do you have anyone?"

This question, even at such a young age, weighed heavily on his chest.

"No," he answered in his little voice.

The gigantic hand of the officer reached out to him. "Come on. Let's get you some real food."

Stepping down off the crate, Shade hesitated to take the man's hand. However, the promise of food gave him hope he'd get more to eat.

He took his outstretched hand, and it changed his life forever.

Slowly coming back to reality, Shade swallowed the lump in his throat. The noise around him was familiar and not at the same time. Even though the memory seemed fresh it had been over twenty years.

Over twenty years?

How had that much time gone by? How he had changed and grown in all those years. Now, he was thirty. The big three-oh. He planned for this birthday to be much different than what it was at the moment. Looking up at the window—one last time—he pulled away from the curb and was off to his next destination.

Shade maneuvered through Buffalo traffic to the restaurant where he and Jenessa first met. This time he parked and actually went inside. Sitting in a booth, he stared at the two tables where his life truly changed.

The waitress came over, and he ordered coffee. His eyes continued to wander over to the area. Many happy memories floated through his mind. All involving Jenessa.

He had wanted their first date to be memorable, but he didn't have much money. Just his left-over student loan money and what little bit he received from his odd jobs. Feeling as if he should take her to the fanciest place in town, he knew he wouldn't be able to. However, he knew how to have fun with a small amount of money.

Their memorable first date ended up being at an arcade. Sure it seemed childish, but Jenessa never complained. In fact, he could still hear her laughter and cheers as she beat him—three times—at air hockey. He had claimed to be distracted by her beauty, which hadn't been a lie. She was the most beautiful being his eyes ever laid on.

"Are you okay?"

The waitress's question made him jerk. "Um…yes. Yes, I'm okay. Thank you." He dropped some money on the table and slid out of the booth and went back to the rental car.

Slowly making his way back to the hotel, he passed the campus. Memories flooded him as he remembered certain buildings with his favorite classes and professors. Then the hockey rink that changed the way he played, and how to handle himself.

Being in foster care and bouncing from place to place, he knew when to keep his head down and when he needed to make his presence known. Shade never liked to fight or even cause problems. Generally, he stayed in the corner and remained alone. He found it easier.

No one believed he would make it in college, but he knew it would be the only way out and to make something of himself. Yes, he lived on his student loans and odd jobs, but it was his only option. When he saw the signs for the hockey walk-on tryouts, he found them to be a bit strange. He figured they wouldn't need walk-ons. But he decided to give it a shot.

His equipment was mismatched, extremely used, and worn out, but he had his stick. The last foster home he was at loved hockey, which is where he received the hand me down equipment.

On the ice, he felt alive and someone or something must have been thinking he deserved a break. Shade played one of his best games, holding his own on the ice better than most on the roster.

He earned a spot.

Shade returned the rental and Uber'd back to the hotel. When he strolled in, Jarvis was in the room watching TV.

"Where have you been?"

"Just needed to be alone." He fell onto his bed.

"Edgar and I were going to take you out to lunch for your birthday."

"Sorry, man," he mumbled, feeling bad. However, he needed time for himself today.

"No big deal. Are you okay?"

Shade sat up. "Yeah. It's okay."

"*It's* okay or *you're* okay?"

He didn't answer because he honestly didn't know the answer.

Jarvis opened his mouth to say something, but a knock at the door stopped him. He got off the bed and opened the door. Shade heard the words *dinner* and glanced down at this watch. He hadn't realized how long he'd been driving around.

"You coming?"

"Go on and save me a spot. I'll be right there," Shade said, feeling his phone vibrating in his pocket.

The name of the divorce lawyer glowed on the screen. "Hello."

"Mr. Wooten, Grant here."

"Grant, how are things coming along?"

"Well."

Shade heard a deep sigh.

"I did the petition just as you asked. I'm holding it to ensure you hadn't changed your mind on anything."

He paused. He hoped Jenessa would have reached out to him by now. Still nothing.

"All I want is my truck and half of the savings account. She can have everything else." He debated about the money, but he didn't want Jenessa to think he was being greedy. Although, it could help him get his own place.

"You know—"

"Yes." Shade cut him off. "I know I don't have to give her everything, but it's what I want to do."

After a few seconds of silence, Grant conceded and said he would get everything ready to file.

When Shade ended the call, he just sat in the quiet room. The tears seemed to bubble up from behind his eyes. He never wanted this. He only ever wanted Jenessa and their marriage. However, he couldn't make her happy anymore.

He had failed.

Failed at the one thing he thought he was good at in

life.

Not being able to sit in the hotel room any longer, since it felt as if the walls were closing in, he went down to the team dinner.

Nova and Janan were like their godfather, Oliver Matthews, in the fact they loved the team being all together as much as possible. Oliver would do many events throughout the season and offseason to gather everyone into one room or place.

Team dinners were just the same.

A buffet-style layout had everything you could ever want. Shade came in at the tail end of the line. Filling his plate, he made his way over to the table where Jarvis, Edgar, Dag, Zerrick, and Walker sat. Jarvis had kept a seat for him.

"Happy birthday, Captain," Zerrick greeted him first.

"Yeah, happy birthday," Walker added.

"Thanks, everyone," Shade said.

The guys were focusing on eating, all thinking about the game in a few hours. Small conversations were happening, but Shade remained quiet. The delicious food held his attention until they began talking to him about the upcoming game.

"All right. Listen up," Hamilton shouted over everyone. "Finish up, get ready, get bags packed. You all know the drill."

The team finished up and did what their coach said. Shade was toward the back of the line when he heard his name. Turning, he saw Cat. He found it a tad strange because even though PR sometimes traveled with the team, the newbies never did.

"Hi, Cat."

"Happy birthday."

He did catch the sultry tone. "Thanks."

"Any big plans *before* your birthday?"

His eyes glanced down as she stuck her chest out. He didn't mean for them to, but they did.

"Captain." Edgar slapped his shoulder. "You can't be late." He guided Shade away from Cat and toward the elevator.

Once they were out of her earshot, in a low tone Edgar said, "Stay away from her."

"Why?"

"Do you know why she's here?"

"No."

"She was sleeping with several Tigers' players. Kian is giving her a second chance but on a probationary period. One *screw* up and she's gone."

Shade furrowed his brow. "Why wasn't she fired?"

Edgar shrugged. "No clue. Just stay away from her. She has the look."

"Look?"

"Don't act like you've not seen her flirting with you," Edgar called him out.

"Okay. Okay." He nodded. He knew she was but was doing his best to ignore it.

"You don't want her, do you?" he questioned.

"I want Jenessa and only her," he firmly stated.

"Then keep it professional and stay in public spots. We don't want any rumors to start."

The elevator came, and they headed up to their rooms. Shade changed into his suit and packed his bag. He scanned the room ensuring he hadn't forgotten any of his items. Jarvis did the same and before long, it was time to get on the bus.

The guys were in game mode. They all remained quiet with their earbuds in or had their eyes closed or were staring straight ahead.

When they made it to the arena, everyone got off the bus and went into the locker room. They changed out of their suits and into their workout outfits. This was the time when they split off and did their own routine. Shade didn't have the same superstitious behavior as many of the others. He just did his thing. He would play two-touch ball with a circle of guys and then worked the bike for a little bit.

He did the same tonight.

After he felt warmed up, he went back into the locker room. For one final time, he checked his phone. Besides Mikayla, Greer, and a few other hockey players, no one else wished him a happy birthday. Especially the one person he wanted to.

Pushing everything out of his mind and thinking only of the game ahead of him, Shade changed into his pads and uniform. A few chatted around him, but he tried his best to keep his thoughts clear.

Hamilton strolled in and began giving them a slight rundown of the night's game plan before releasing them to warm up on the ice. Shade left the room last since he was the captain. That was a Bears' tradition that started many, many years ago.

On the ice, Shade was free. Nothing matters to him but winning. Stretching his muscles, he watched around him. Everyone had on their game face. There were a few laughing and joking around. Getting up, he skated, did some stick handling skills, and shot the puck toward the net. On the other side of the glass stood numerous fans with signs, all trying to gain the players' attention. Shade noticed several signs wishing him a happy birthday. Everyone knew he had been born and raised in Buffalo. When he was drafted, many local news channels gave him the media name of 'hometown boy' and told his tragic story. It stuck to him to that day. A few of the signs said the same.

After tossing a few pucks into the stands, he left the ice and headed back to the locker room. Soon the rest of the team came in and Hamilton gave them the game plan, again, and sent them back out to the ice. At the back of the line, Shade closed his eyes and listened to the music and crowd. Home crowds really let loose for their team.

On the ice, he skated around the net and then lined up for the national anthems. Since they played both, Shade kept his eyes closed, taking deep breaths and trying to focus on the game in front of him. As the signer completed the anthem, the crowd went wild and the Bears lined up for the puck to drop. Shade skated back to his defensive stand. He watched the refs hand, not blinking until the puck hit the ice and Finlay Mackey snagged it and passed it to his right. Then they were off. For the first period, the Bears fought hard, but Buffalo wanted it more. Scoring on Liam.

Twice.

When the team went back to the locker room, Shade told Liam to shake it off. He didn't want Liam to become discouraged.

"This fucking sucks," he growled, dropping into his stall.

Shade slapped his padded shoulder. "There's still a lot of game left. Let it go and get ready for the next period."

Liam looked up at him. "You're right. You're right."

"You good?"

Liam nodded, and Shade went to his stall. Hamilton came in several minutes later with an updated game plan. Everyone put all their attention on Hamilton. When he finished, the team, especially Shade, were fired up and ready to be back on the ice.

As intermission finished and the Bears came out of the tunnel the crowd was deafening for the Buffalo squad coming out. Shade shut out the noise. Determination pulsed through him. His body was tight, ready to score.

And that was what he did.

And again…

And again…

Defensive players didn't normally get hat tricks. Shade

only had two in his entire career. Tonight would be his third. He barely remembered scoring but celebrated as if he did.

When the final buzzer sounded, the entire team celebrated. Helmet bumps, shoulder slaps, and sticks slapped on his leg pads came from every teammate. Once in the locker room, the coaching staff gave their congratulations. Shade barely remembered everything happening around him before they were loading up onto the bus and heading to the airport.

Once settled into his seat, reality overtook him. The plane was heading back to Manchester, but no one would be waiting for him at the airport. No families would be there because they would be landing so late, but Jenessa used to stay awake for him. Especially, after a big win or a big game for him.

Sadness washed over him as he stared out the window. He had felt alone for the past three years, but at that very moment, he never felt more alone. Not when his mother left. Not when he bounced from foster home to foster home. Just the moment when he stared out into the darkness of the sky, seeing the spattering of lights thousands of feet below him.

He was alone.

CHAPTER TEN
Jenessa

Putting the picture frames into the box, Jenessa thought she'd be more emotional. This job had consumed her for the past three years. It had been her first true job after law school. She planned to be a partner someday.

But today, she quit.

Two days ago, Jenessa's eyes were glued to the TV as she watched Shade score a hat trick on his birthday. The pure joy on his face made her feel crushed and happy. He did better without her. She had wanted him to be happy again, but it hurt at the same time.

Nonetheless, seeing him triggered something deep inside her. A feeling she had hidden and never addressed. Especially in the last three years.

"Is there anything I can help you with?" Tiffany asked softly as she stepped into the office.

"No." Jenessa gave her a genuine smile. "I'm all done."

"I hate you're leaving," she confessed.

"It's time." She nodded, double-checking the drawers of her desk.

"I understand."

Jenessa stopped and looked up. There were tears in Tiffany's eyes. "You'll be fine and if you ever need a reference..." There wasn't a need to finish the sentence. She knew what she meant to Jenessa.

"Thank you."

Lifting the box, she gave her now previous assistant another smile and left.

Walking into the quiet house she set down the box and her purse. Looking around she wondered what to do next. She had no clue. Sitting on the sectional in the den, her mind raced. She was unemployed. She had no prospects or job offers.

Nothing.

Dropping her head into her hands, she tried not to let the panic overtake her. She thought back to the reason why she came up with this crazy notion. When she shut off the TV after Shade's outstanding game, she cried.

The tears were from years of pain and frustration and from being a failure. Everything from the last three years of hiding it all away finally bubbled over. By the time the tears stopped, she was curled up in fetal position on the floor. She didn't even know how she ended up there. But she saw things clearer.

Hiding in her office only brought her heartache. Jenessa remembered the days where she laughed, joked, smiled. Days laying in bed with Shade making love, talking about everything and nothing. Just being happy.

She needed to find herself again.

"Nes!" Mikayla's voice carried through the house.

"Here," she called, wiping her face of the few escaped tears on her cheeks.

"What the hell?" she exclaimed entering the room, holding up her cell phone.

"What?" Jenessa confusingly stared at the blank screen.

"You quit? You quit your job?" The disbelief and

bewilderment clearly covered her face and was heard in her voice.

"I did," she confirmed.

Waking up this morning she knew today would be the day to quit. Her first thought was to text Shade and tell him, but she knew she couldn't. They hadn't spoken in several weeks. So, she told Mikayla.

"Would you care to explain to me why? And before you do, let me say how happy I am that you did." Mikayla sat next to her.

"I need...something." Jenessa couldn't find the right wording to express herself.

"Something?"

Taking a deep breath, she felt the heaviness on her chest. As if a brick house landed on it. Mikayla took her hand, giving it a tender squeeze.

"I don't know who I am without my work. I've been hiding behind it for the longest time. I've forgotten who I am. But since I left the office, I have no clue what to do next." Some of the weight came off her chest as she spoke.

"You're Jenessa Wooten. Wife of Shade and sister to the most incredible person in the world. Me. And I'm an outstanding person."

Jenessa rested her head on Mikayla's shoulder and giggled. "You're a nut." She didn't respond to the part of being Shade's wife.

"I am, but you're stuck with me," she replied.

She felt they were growing close again. Many times she held onto Mikayla's strength. Even though she was strong, Mikayla sat at a different level.

"It's okay to try to find yourself again."

Jenessa rose up. "I know, but I feel lost."

"Which means you'll find your way soon."

Letting the words sink in, she wondered if they would come true. Things didn't seem to be looking up for her. No job. No husband. Thinking back when Shade was on road games, she had no problem being alone. In fact, she enjoyed it at times. She and Mikayla would hang out and do things together. Shopping. Dinners. Road trips. Girls' weekends. Then an idea popped in her head.

"Kay, let's go to Vegas," Jenessa blurted out.

"Excuse me?" Mikayla's eyes went wide.

"Right now. Today, let's get on a plane and spend a few days there." She spoke fast and couldn't be sure if her words made sense.

"Huh?" Now a furrowed brow appeared. "You just want to hop on a plane and go to Las Vegas?"

"Yes. Let's go crazy. Be wild. Let loose. Go shopping. Get drunk. Just…go." The excitement overtook her with all the ideas spinning in her head.

"Hold on." Mikayla waved her hands around. "Who are you? And what did you do with *my* sister?"

"I'm serious." Jenessa had a firm tone to get her point across. "I need this."

Studying her face, she didn't say anything. Instead, she pulled out her phone and tapped the screen numerous times.

"There's a nonstop leaving in five hours from Boston. Hurry up and pack," Mikayla informed her.

Jenessa squealed and hugged Mikayla before racing up the stairs. Tossing clothes into a small luggage case, Mikayla yelled she was going to pack and would be back within the hour. Grabbing her bathroom items her cheeks hurt from smiling.

This would be great.

They managed to get to Boston in plenty of time to board the plane. Albeit, security had been backed up. The flight had been uneventful. They spent their time trying to find a hotel. Jenessa left it up to Mikayla since her hidden talent was finding outstanding deals.

Once the plane landed in Nevada, they grabbed a cab to the hotel. Just as Jenessa thought, Mikayla found an outstanding deal right on the strip. They checked in and went up to the room.

"I say we get changed and grab some dinner. I'm starving," Jenessa suggested as she opened her bag and pulled out some items.

"Me too," she agreed, unzipping her case.

Jenessa went into the bathroom to freshen up. They weren't going anywhere fancy, just casual fun. She figured her emotions would be everywhere, but a small sense of calm floated around her. The first time in…well, she didn't know how long.

Opening the door, she heard Mikayla talking to someone on her phone.

"I mean, she just up and quit her job. I don't know what is going on, but I'm in Vegas, and she needs me."

She paused.

"I don't know how long we'll be here, and I don't care. I won't let her do this alone."

Jenessa hung her head. Her sister had to be the toughest person in the world yet had the biggest heart. Holding the door, the calm left and was replaced with sadness. Like Shade, Mikayla had received the same treatment from Jenessa.

"I love you too, Jarvis. Let Shade know she's fine. I know he's worrying."

Those words made her breath catch. Shade worried about her. Why? Why did he still even care?

"Just tell him," Mikayla repeated. "I love you."

The call must have ended because she heard Mikayla moving around and she wasn't talking anymore. Jenessa walked out as if she hadn't been eavesdropping.

"You look great," Mikayla commented.

"Bathroom's all yours." She glanced at the full-length mirror near the closet. A pair of dark skinny jeans hugged her waist. She slipped into a long sleeve, light cotton deep purple shirt. She had a matching pair of ballet flats. Her hair sat high in a messy bun on top of her head. Even though she normally wore makeup, tonight she just had on a little bit of mascara and gloss.

Sitting on the bed, she picked up her cell phone and debated calling Shade. Staring at the screen, her finger almost touched the green phone icon but stopped, she then tossed the phone onto the bed. This weekend was about her. She needed to clear her head and not think about Shade, their marriage, being jobless, and their baby.

When Mikayla came out, she was wearing a pair of straight jeans and a red oversized off the shoulder sweater. Her flawless makeup made her beauty stand out even more. Without saying anything she came over to Jenessa and hugged her.

"What's this for?"

"Because you're the best big sister." Mikayla released her.

Tears welled up in Jenessa's eyes. "No, I'm not."

Kneeling in front of her, she said, "Yes, you are. You just need to come to terms that we're here for you, and you can't do it all alone."

Saying nothing, Jenessa avoided eye contact. She did that when she wanted to pretend the truth wasn't staring at her.

"Come on." Mikayla stood. "I found this great bar and grill on Yelp. I say we load up on greasy bar food and drink our weight in some craft beer."

As she finished, Jenessa's stomach growled on cue.

"I'm going to say it's a yes."

The Uber dropped them off and they strolled into the packed bar. Jenessa expected it to be rundown and grimy. However, this one had an upper class feel to it. More upscale than the ones she'd visited.

The hostess, another content Jenessa had been surprised to see, escorted them to a booth. The hostess handed them both a menu with a hard wooden backing and pointed to the drink menus at the end of the table.

"I feel as if I'm very underdressed." Jenessa glanced around at the other patrons.

"Agreed. I thought the words 'bar and grill' would mean casual," Mikayla commented, opening the menu. "This isn't your typical bar food."

Jenessa flipped her menu open and saw exactly what she meant. These weren't greasy appetizers, burgers, and the normal deep-fried finger food. These items came out of a five-star restaurant.

"Welcome, ladies. What can I start you off with?" The waitress stepped up to their table.

"Are you feeling adventurous?" Mikayla questioned Jenessa, shutting the menu.

She wondered where she was going with the question but decided to hell with it. "Yes, we're in Vegas. Where else can we be crazy?"

"Great." She beamed. "Neither of us are allergic to anything and want to try the best you have. You pick it." She instructed the waitress.

"How many courses?" she asked with her pen at the ready.

"Three," Mikayla answered.

"Beer, well drinks, or something different?"

"Beer."

"Price range?"

"None."

"I'll be back shortly." The waitress smiled and walked away.

"I don't think I've ever let the wait staff pick my food," Jenessa admitted.

"Why not? They know what's good, and it's fun not having to decide," Mikayla answered.

"You know when Shade goes through a drive-thru, he just says 'give me a number one.' without even knowing what it is." Jenessa laughed at the memory of him doing it.

"He's weird," Mikayla joined in.

"He would say the number one is the bestseller, so it had to be good." She remembered having the conversation with him time and time again, never understanding the point of it.

"So, we're here, what else do you want to do?" Mikayla inquired.

Jenessa got the feeling she wanted to change the topic. "I figured we get some shopping in. Maybe a spa day?"

"Sounds good to me. I need to update my wardrobe a bit."

"Being with Mr. Model causes you to stay away from all the black outfits," she teased.

"Not all of it. He enjoys my black crotchless lingerie." Mikayla winked.

"Really? You're going to tell me about your sex life." Jenessa rolled her eyes.

"Why not? I'm sure you're dying to know."

Jenessa shook her head. "No, I'm not."

"Bet I could teach you some new tricks," she quipped.

Jenessa was certain she could. It had been three years since she and Shade had any form of intimacy.

"All right, ladies." The waitress returned. "I've brought you our vegan potato skins. These are organic potatoes with soy cheese and soy bacon."

She set the plate in the middle of the table. They weren't the normal boat size portion one would get from a normal bar and grill. These were small petite potatoes with a teeny amount of cheese and a bacon bit size of bacon on top.

"The beer is a berry-infused light beer. The sweetness cuts the saltiness of the appetizer." She placed the beer on the table. "Enjoy," she said before strolling away.

Jenessa and Mikayla eyed the beer. One would expect it

to be in a larger beer glass but not this place. The glass couldn't hold more than six ounces. Tops.

"Maybe we should have chosen the eight dollar buffet in the hotel restaurant." Mikayla picked up her glass, inspecting it as if more would magically appear.

"They're just giving out the recommended portions." Jenessa came up with an excuse.

"Well, this New Englander needs the big girl portions."

Jenessa began laughing. Mikayla always had a way with words.

"Let's try it out. Maybe they're small because the next course will be bigger." She wiped the laughter tears from her eyes.

"Hope so," Mikayla muttered before sipping the beer. "Now, this is delicious."

They munched on the bite-size potatoes, which weren't bad, as Mikayla discussed her job because Jenessa had asked about it. Pride filled her as Mikayla told her about the new designs she'd been working on. Jenessa didn't have a talent. Unless you counted arguing. She had that trait mastered.

The waitress brought their next course and Mikayla almost cheered seeing larger portions.

"Who would like the Philly chicken and who would enjoy the California sunrise burger?"

Glancing at each other, they questioned which one they would want and what was in them.

"The California sunrise burger is a grass-fed burger with organic cheese. On top is a range-free egg and an avocado," the waitress explained.

"I'll take it," Mikayla said.

The waitress handed out the plates and told us there was a side of sweet potato fries with it.

"It looks good," Jenessa commented, studying her plate.

"I've also given you lovely ladies a crisp light beer with a hint of citrus to keep your palette fresh." She put the drinks down in front of them.

When she left, Jenessa quickly cut the sandwich. A Philly generally came on a sub but this sat on large sourdough bread. They ate quietly for several minutes. Jenessa didn't even think of all the calories and carbs she currently was devouring. It tasted too good to care about it.

"Oh, man, this is the best." Mikayla moaned in between bites.

"It is," she agreed, taking another large bite.

"This beer is great too."

Again, Jenessa nodded. "She did an outstanding job."

"See, I told you. Sometimes it's fun to be adventurous every once and a while." Mikayla shot her a fun glare.

"Fine. You're right," she conceded.

"I know." She gave her a sweet wink before popping a fry into her mouth. "So, when are we going to talk about you?"

Jenessa stopped midbite. "Do you really want to hear the nothings in my head?" She hoped she would ask anything else, but she knew her better than that.

"Yes," she spoke clearly and firmly.

Taking a bite, it bought her several seconds to figure out what to say, or where to begin.

"You're not alone, Nes," Mikayla spoke softly. "Even when you're a royal bitch, I'll always be here for you."

She set down the sandwich and wiped her hands with a thick linen napkin. Memories of them talking for hours about everything and nothing came flooding back.

"We used to be close," Jenessa said without really thinking about it.

"We're still close and always will be. You're the one to push everyone away and close yourself off to the world," she told her.

As much as she wanted to argue, she couldn't because it was the truth. She leaned back in the booth and sipped her beer. Not sure where to start, Jenessa kept her focus around the restaurant.

"Just tell me one thing you're thinking about. Just one." Mikayla placed her arms on the table bringing herself closer.

Before she said anything, the waitress returned to check on them.

"Could you bring us four shots of tequila?" Jenessa asked.

"Sure." The waitress smiled.

"Are we turning things up here, Nes?" Mikayla inquired.

"If we're going to discuss me, then yes." She pushed her plate to the side.

"Okay." She nodded, moving her plate as well, waiting for her to speak.

Jenessa knew, deep down, she had to release all the emotions hidden far away. Telling Mikayla would be best. Yes, she'd give her opinion, but in the end, she wouldn't be judging her too harshly. No matter how much they argued, Mikayla was right. They would be sisters for life.

The waitress returned with a small tray. Placing it in the middle of the table it had four large shot glasses, several limes in a small bowl, and packets of salt. They handed over their plates of half-eaten food to give themselves more room.

Mikayla and Jenessa prepped their first shot. Clinking their glasses together, they knocked back the clear alcohol.

"I'm failing." Jenessa slightly slammed the shot glass down.

"At what?"

"Everything." She placed the lime into her mouth, sucking out the bitter juice.

"Name one thing?"

Discarding the lime, she let the alcohol warm her blood before answering. "For one, my marriage."

"Your marriage hasn't failed. You're too stubborn to pick up the phone and talk to Shade," Mikayla informed her.

She didn't agree, even though she was right. *Again.*

"If you two would sit down and talk, then I know you both can work this all out," she continued.

"All of it might be true, but he's doing much better without me. Why would I ruin it?" Jenessa felt the tears bubbling up.

"You're a fool." Mikayla shook her head in frustration.

"Look at it from my point of view. He's smiling, racking up points and hell they even made him captain. Would any of it happened if he stayed with me?" She hoped Mikayla understood her words.

"Nes, you're seeing it so wrong. He may have smiled when he scored his hat trick, but it's not a real one. It's for show. He's barely grinned since leaving you. The reason the points are racking up is because he works out and goes to practice. Nothing else. He misses you. He's trying to give you space, and until you call him, he's not going to contact you."

Jenessa turned away from her hard glare. She had nothing to say because she didn't want to imagine Shade sitting and waiting by the phone. Picking up the other shot glass, she swallowed down the drink. This time she didn't use the salt or lime to ensure the burn would last. She hoped it would take away some of her pain.

It did not.

"Why did you really quit your job?" Mikayla moved away from the Shade topic.

"Because I had to." She paused trying to figure out what she would say next. "I've been using work as a shield. It kept me from dealing with everything around me. Especially the hurt." Her eyes blurred from the tears creeping up.

Mikayla reached over and took her hand, holding onto it tightly.

"Are we doing dessert?" The waitress appeared at their table.

"Yes," Jenessa answered. "And more tequila."

"And a couple of glasses of water," Mikayla added.

As the waitress left, Jenessa remained quiet, unsure of what else there was to say or how her sister felt.

"Hiding in my office, I kept the pain away. Typing motions allowed me to forget the loss. Taking more cases and increasing my workload helped me ignore Shade." Now the tears fell, gently sliding down her cheeks.

The waitress set another small tray of tequila and two large slices of double chocolate cake. "I brought some napkins as well," she said softly before leaving them alone.

"I guess I look bad," Jenessa mumbled picking up a napkin and dabbing the wetness away.

"You're beautiful," Mikayla spoke with a crack in her voice.

"I'm almost thirty."

"And?"

"I thought everything would be different," she whispered.

"Jenessa, I can't imagine the pain you were or are going through. I lost my nephew, but you lost your son. However, you forget Shade lost his son too. He remained strong for you, but he needed you too. He needed to break down and have someone to lean on as well. Did you not realize how bad he was feeling? How much he needed you too?"

The tears rolled faster. "Shade didn't—"

"Yes." Mikayla cut her off. "I listened to the strongest man I've ever known cry in a bathroom all the time for three years. He didn't think I heard him, but I did. He never shed a tear in front of you because he wanted to be strong for you."

Jenessa felt her brow furrow deeply. "What are you talking about? Shade has never cried."

"What part is tripping you up? The part where Shade needed his wife to lean on? Or the part where he's a father who lost his son?"

Even through her sister's sarcastic tone, Jenessa's heart broke. Even more so than before. She pictured Shade sitting on their bathroom floor crying alone.

Every time she would break down, he would be there. Several times, she let him hold her. But it didn't take long before she shut down the tears and pushed him—and everyone—away.

"I guess I really am a royal bitch." She picked up another napkin and wiped away more of the tears.

"You can fix this. You can get back to your life. The one you and Shade were always meant to have." Mikayla's firm tone hit her hard.

Without saying anything, Jenessa grabbed the single shot Mikayla hadn't taken and knocked it back. Then another. The burn subsided faster with each shot.

"Drinking isn't the answer right now."

She didn't comment. Even though she wanted to finish the shots she said she was ready to leave. Mikayla called the waitress over and asked for the check. Jenessa slid out of the booth. It took her a second as the tequila rushed through her, then she went outside. She hoped for cooler air, but the desert heat was thick, even in November. She continued to blink hard, trying to make sure no more tears fell.

The more Mikayla had talked, the more reality set in. The more she could feel the true pain she put Shade through. She knew before, but now it slapped her in the face. Shade should have left years ago. He deserved happiness, and she couldn't give it to him.

"The Uber is almost here."

Jenessa jumped at Mikayla's voice. "How long have you been there?"

"A minute or two. You seemed lost in thought."

"I just want to go back to the hotel."

As if the universe listened to her request, the car pulled up. They both got in and didn't speak. She knew Mikayla was giving her space and appreciated it. When they were dropped off and made their way to the room, Jenessa thought only of Shade. Many memories. Most of which were happy ones. She and Shade joking around, watching movies curled up together, laying in bed. Just being together and in love.

Kicking off her shoes, she fell onto the bed and passed out.

Jenessa woke long before Mikayla. She decided to hit the hotel gym. Surprisingly, she remembered to pack a set of workout attire. Jumping on the elliptical, she popped in her earbuds and turned on an audiobook. As much as she loved fictional books, she ended up picking out a self-improvement book. Never really buying into the 'self-help' movement, this book just happened to catch her attention.

Picking up speed she listened intently to the narrator's words. Thinking the book would be a simple, mundane bore, she shockingly became wrapped up and lost within the words. The first couple chapters didn't mean much to her, but by the third chapter the subject manner seemed to be written just for her and her current situation.

After ninety minutes, when her legs hurt and burned and sweat stung her eyes, she decided to stop. Stepping off the machine the narrator spoke to her soul.

"It's okay to grieve. It's not okay to stop living."

Grabbing a gym towel, she patted away the sweat and returned to the room. Mikayla still laid wrapped in the blankets and was fast asleep. Jenessa decided to get ready, figuring her sister would wake soon. The words from the book continued to spin in her head as the cool water from the shower calmed her body.

She decided she would go casual. This was her vacation, or somewhat of one, and she had no real desire to doll herself up. She dried her hair and twisted it up to a messy bun. Slapping on tinted moisture, she then dressed in a pair of capris that were a bit too tight in the thighs. She blamed it on the beer and carbs from last night. Deciding on a loose T-shirt, she double-checked herself in the mirror. She looked tired but that seemed to be a normal appearance for her.

Walking out of the bathroom, Mikayla was sitting on the side of the bed, drinking a cup of coffee.

"I made one for you." She nodded over to the table the TV sat on.

"Thanks." Jenessa picked up the cup and sat next to her. "And thank you for last night."

Mikayla looked at her. "You need to talk, Nes. I'm here. I'm a good listener, but above all, I love you and when you hurt, I do too."

"I think you need to get ready, and we need to hit the stores." Jenessa stood up and went to her bed. Right now, she didn't want to cry this early in the day. "I need to have a good day today." She hadn't meant to say it out loud.

Mikayla stood, kissed Jenessa on the forehead and said, "Then I'll make sure it'll happen."

There were many times Mikayla took the big sister role and it used to bother her, but at times, she appreciated it. Her stepping up took the weight off Jenessa's shoulder.

She made her second cup of coffee as Mikayla came out of the bathroom. The girl could get ready quickly and look like she spent three hours. However, she had a natural beauty, even with her dyed black hair.

"Want to grab some brunch before we max out our credit card?" Mikayla slid her foot into her pink booties that matched her black and pink T-shirt dress.

"Yes, let's just hit the hotel restaurant." Jenessa grabbed her purse and phone, as did Mikayla, and they headed out the door.

The brunch was delicious and the discussion between them was light and fun. Mikayla told her how great she and Jarvis were doing. Hearing about her relationship did bring a smile to her face because those two had been chasing each other for years. Even though they pretended not to know each other when they were in the same room, everyone around them knew.

When they finished they started their shopping spree. Hitting the higher-end stores first. Jenessa purchased a couple of new pairs of heels and a new purse. They Uber'd over to the mall, and Jenessa ended up getting a few outfits as did Mikayla.

"I think we should go clubbing tonight," Jenessa suggested.

"Clubbing?" Mikayla stopped browsing through the racks and stared at her. "You?"

"What? I used to when I went to college," she told her.

"I don't think happy hour at Applebee's counts." Mikayla rolled her eyes.

"Hey." She sounded offended by her comment. "I did go out with my friends. Not a lot, but a few times." Normally, she spent time with Shade before going off to law school. Then she would spend a lot of time on the phone with him.

"Maybe we'll go to a nice lounge or something?" Mikayla suggested.

"No. Come on, Kay. Let's get our groove on." Jenessa began to dance a bit.

"Oh my God, don't do that ever again." Mikayla started to move away from her.

"Kay," she begged. "We've never gone together. We're in Vegas. I bet we could get an appointment at the salon, dress to impress, and hit the town." She beamed, hoping her sister would agree.

"Who are you trying to impress? Your husband is in New Hampshire."

The words actually hurt her. Almost as if she slapped her. Immediately, she shut down.

"Let's go back." Turning on her heel, she began heading out of the store. She continued even when

Mikayla called out her name.

Jenessa was quite a bit away from the store when she caught up to her.

"Stop walking." She stood in front of her, making Jenessa come to a halt. "I'm sorry."

"You don't like to apologize," Jenessa snapped.

"True, but I went too far. You know I don't think before I speak."

She couldn't argue because it was Mikayla's superpower to be unfiltered.

"I don't want to think about Shade, or my unemployment, or Clay, or anything else right now." She raised her voice as the words rushed out.

"I understand. You know what we're in Vegas and we *should* go out."

"Now, you're just patronizing me," she groaned as Mikayla used almost the same words she had said. Trying to move around her, she continued to block her path.

"I'm not. I want to. We've not really clubbed together and what a better place than Vegas," Mikayla said with a softer expression. "We'll get trashed and dance the night away."

Even though it was Jenessa's idea, it sounded like the perfect night when she said it. Normally, she would never suggest going to a club, but what she said next surprised her even more.

"I need a dress."

Jenessa studied her little, sparkly black dress. Turning left and then right, she checked herself from every angle. The high-end fashion dress cost her a lot. However, she purchased it just for this evening. It clung to her curves and stopped mid-thigh. The sleeves started at the wrist and touched the top of her shoulders, cutting into a deep sweetheart neckline. The top of her chest and collarbones were completely exposed. She felt pretty hot.

Mikayla strolled out of the bathroom in a deep purple silk A-line cocktail dress. She could stop traffic. Her black hair laid in soft waves down her back and her makeup looked like perfection. She could walk any runway and steal the entire show.

"I've booked us a VIP booth."

Taking a few seconds to process what Mikayla said, Jenessa just nodded.

"I want to drink the night away," she said picking up her clutch.

"The car is waiting." She grabbed her tiny purse, and they both headed out of the hotel room.

Mikayla informed her she ordered a car service instead of just an Uber. They weren't going to just some club. This place was listed as the hottest place in Vegas. Exclusive to celebrities and top-notch athletes. As Mikayla called them "The Ballers". Jenessa explained it wasn't the best term to describe them.

"It does tonight," Mikayla told her as they got into the Audi SUV with a very large driver. He could almost double as a bodyguard.

The drive hadn't been as long as Jenessa imagined it would be. A massive line of patrons stood along a rope barrier. She felt displeased about standing in the line for the majority of the night. The driver stopped the vehicle at the front door curb and rushed to get the doors for them.

Mikayla immediately strolled up to the doorman who held a tablet. "Kay-Kay, plus one," she said, not asking if they were on the list.

"Welcome." The doorman's deep voice greeted them, and he opened the door for them.

"Kay-Kay?" she questioned once inside the posh lobby.

She answered with a shrug and nothing more.

"I've never heard anyone call you Kay-Kay," Jenessa continued.

"You're not with me twenty-four-seven," she countered and walked further into the club.

Jenessa followed her and acted as if she belonged there. Clearly, she didn't because everyone around her was much younger and much hotter. At least, she thought so. Maybe she was too old to be clubbing. As they fully stepped into the club, the music thumped loudly. She worried her heart would fall out of rhythm. Mikayla reached down and gripped her hand, leading her through the packed crowd. Jenessa couldn't figure out how she knew where to go, but after a minute, they were going up to the second floor. Again, she gave the name of Kay-Kay and the bouncer told her which table was theirs.

Once they sat in a super comfortable love seat, Jenessa glanced out to the crowd below them. A very sexy waitress came up to them.

"What can I get you ladies?" she asked loudly to be heard over the music.

"Dirty martini," Mikayla spoke first.

"Cosmo," Jenessa said next.

"Be right back," she told them with a smile.

Leaning back on the love seat, Jenessa studied the crowd of people. They were all having a blast, laughing and drinking.

"What's wrong?" Mikayla questioned, moving closer so she could be heard.

"I'm old," she answered.

Her sister laughed. "You're almost thirty. Not a hundred."

"Feels the same."

"You're being a bit dramatic." Mikayla continued to laugh.

"This wasn't the plan," she said.

"You wanted to come to a club," she reminded her.

"No." She shook her head. "I mean my life, in general."

"What was your plan?" Mikayla inquired.

Before she could answer, the waitress came back with their drinks.

"Keep 'em coming," Mikayla told her and turned back to Jenessa. "I have an idea."

"What?"

"How about you drop all your defenses? Drop them all and talk. Tell me everything. I'll just sit here and listen."

Staring at Mikayla for a few seconds she wondered if she ever could do it. Since Clay's death, she put up so many walls to keep everyone out and not face her reality.

"Just for this night." Mikayla sipped her drink, reiterating the proposition.

Jenessa picked up her drink that sat on the small table in front of them. She took to large gulps, mulling over the idea. She knew she had a lot to say and should get it off her chest. All her pain weighed so heavily on her.

"I figured when I was thirty, Shade and I would be together. Happy. He'd be playing hockey. I'd be home with my career. We'd have at least two kids." The mere mention of children stung at her. "I'd be taking them to little hockey league games while still trying to become partner of the firm."

She took another big drink as her perfect life played out in her head.

"I figured he would retire around thirty-five," she continued. "He would help out with the kids. Maybe coach their hockey teams. He was always good at marketing and advertising. He'd get a job in one of those fields."

Mikayla sipped her drink saying nothing as Jenessa talked.

"Now, look at me. I'm unemployed. Shade's gone. Our son is…" She trailed off powerless to finish the sentence. "I've fucked it all up." She downed the rest of her drink and set the empty glass on the table.

As she promised, she remained silent. It began to irritate Jenessa.

"I know you're dying to say something, Kay. Say it."

116

The waitress came with another round of drinks and Mikayla finished hers in a couple of big gulps.

"You didn't fuck up anything," she started. "Shade wants everything you want and only with you. Clay's death was the most tragic of accidents. An *accident*. I know you hold the responsibility for his death, but it wasn't your fault. You and Shade can have more kids and still keep Clay's memory alive. You can have your dream. You have to talk to Shade to get it. If you both would just sit down and talk. Open up to him and then you need to listen to him."

Nothing she said hadn't been something Jenessa already thought of a million times. Nonetheless, she couldn't believe how simple it sounded.

"I'm his mom. My one job was to protect my son. Especially inside the womb," she blurted out. "What kind of mother doesn't protect her child?"

"You're going to be an outstanding mother. The best. I know it," Mikayla countered. Even over the loud music, she could hear the softness in her tone. "Clay's death was tragic. I know I said it a hundred times, but it's the truth. The next baby you and Shade have will come out perfectly healthy. You both will be the most amazing parents. You just have to talk to Shade. It's the first step."

Jenessa chugged her second drink as if it were in a shot glass and not a martini glass as she let her sister's words sink in. She wanted to be a mother more than anything. Carrying Clay had been an experience she couldn't put into words. Even though she had been very ill the first few months she loved being pregnant. Many times she would have certain food cravings, and Shade rushed off to get her anything she asked for. Never complaining. Even if he'd been tired. He even rubbed her feet and back without her even asking. He constantly told her how beautiful she was, even when she complained about the stretch marks or silly little things about her appearance.

"I love Shade."

The truthful confession left her lips before she could even think about stopping them.

"He loves you. He's broken without you," Mikayla reminded her.

"Our marriage is broken," Jenessa said as the waitress came and set down another round of drinks for them.

"Your marriage might be slightly broken but completely fixable. Just call him and tell him you want to talk," Mikayla told her in a demanding tone.

"I want to. I'm scared." Again, the words flowed from her easily.

"Do you even know how terrified I was to tell Jarvis I loved him after all the mistakes I made with him? Do you even know how much better I felt once I said the words? My heart might have been ripped to shreds, but at least he knew the truth, and I'd never have to play the 'what if' game. Look at us now."

Jenessa didn't know Mikayla had the ability to become scared. She never showed it before. However, her confession meant a lot to Jenessa. Seeing this side of her younger sister showed how much she'd grown. A small ping of hurt and regret hit her. When did she become mature? How did she miss it? Then she remembered how she'd been treating her the past three years.

"For tonight, let's forget the outside world." Jenessa suggested this insane idea in hopes she wouldn't burst into tears.

"So, instead of talking, you want to get completely trashed and not face what's happening around you?"

She nodded at Mikayla, who summed up her idea perfectly. She craved this night to forget she'll need to sit down and face Shade when she arrived back in New Hampshire.

"All right then. Let's get fucked up." Mikayla beamed.

When the waitress came back Mikayla ordered a small tray of shooters. Jenessa had heard of these but was unsure what they were exactly. She didn't want to ask because it would make her look silly. Plus, she trusted her. Picking up her drink she took a sip of it. A few moments later a tray of ten test tubes appeared. There was red liquor inside them.

"These are called cherry lifesavers. They're very sweet and give a quick buzz," Mikayla explained.

She already felt the alcohol working as Mikayla handed her one of the test tubes.

"Cheers." Mikayla held up the tube, opened her mouth, and swallowed the shot down.

Jenessa followed suit and the overly sweet concoction made her lips pucker. Before she knew it, another one appeared in her hand.

And another…

And another…

And another…

Soon she felt great as she finished her cosmo as well. Mikayla seemed to get the giggles and began telling bad *dad* jokes out of nowhere. Jenessa joined in the laughter until her side hurt. She truly didn't know why the lame jokes were funny, but she did.

The waitress continued to bring the drinks but no more shooters. Mikayla asked the waitress how to request a song to the DJ. She informed them they could text a certain number and he would play it. Mikayla grabbed her phone and texted the DJ several song choices. Then she began taking pictures of them. Jenessa smiled, puckered her lips, and acted completely silly with each photo in between laughing again.

As the songs Mikayla requested began to play, they danced up in their area. Jenessa knew she was the world's worst dancer. However, with as much alcohol as she drank, she could not care less.

Her head spun as she continued to move with the music. Too wrapped up, she never noticed Mikayla had been filming her. When she spun around, the waitress had two glasses of water on her tray and even handed one to

Jenessa.

After swallowing it down like the shooters, she grabbed Mikayla's water and did the same thing.

"Come on. The car is here," Mikayla announced.

"I'm not ready," Jenessa whined.

"I am. It's almost three in the morning." She turned the cell phone around and pointed at the time.

"But we're having fun," Jenessa exclaimed.

"*But* it's late and if we leave now, we can get nachos."

Gasping, Jenessa immediately clapped and jumped up and down in place. "Yes, food." She saw Mikayla rolling her eyes at her outburst.

Jenessa had to lean against her as they made their way out of the club and to the car. Once inside, the alcohol hit her hard. Her vision blurred, and she continually giggled at nothing.

"Nes, are you going to be okay?"

She heard the question but was completely unable to process an informative answer. Closing her eyes, her world drifted away.

When Jenessa opened her eyes, she glanced around and realized she was on the bed in their hotel room. Instead of Mikayla being in her bed, she was curled up next to her. She couldn't remember anything after she got into the car. However, someone—certainly her sister—had removed her dress. Currently, she was wearing one of her favorite nightgowns.

As she began to move cautiously, worrying how bad she would feel, her mouth tasted like nasty sandpaper and her head throbbed. Overall, she was not as horrific as she would have figured. Making her way to the bathroom, Mikayla had written a message on the mirror.

"Water in the fridge and aspirin on top of the table."

After she finished in there, she went to get the water and aspirin. Now, Mikayla sat up in the bed.

"How are you feeling?"

"Not as bad as I thought." Jenessa popped the pills in her mouth and cracked open the cold water.

"We're going to be leaving this afternoon," she informed her.

"Why? Do you need to go back?" Jenessa climbed back into the bed.

"No, and since you asked, I'm figuring you don't remember our talk last night," she said.

"The last thing I remember is getting into the car and leaving the club."

"Glad I recorded it then." She reached for her phone and tapped the screen. She turned it around to show Jenessa.

Taking a second for her to focus, it was her on the screen. She had a plate full of nachos on her lap as she sat on the floor of the room.

"I love Shade," Jenessa said before shoving nachos in her mouth. "When I get home, I'm going to tell him how sorry I am. And, and, and, then tell him I was a bitch. A big bitch. But I won't do it anymore. I won't be anymore if he comes home with me."

"What else are you going to tell him?" Mikayla asked out of frame.

Jenessa couldn't answer because she burst into tears. Then the camera moved as Mikayla came over to her and sat down. Jenessa had been saying something, but it was drunken mumbles, and she couldn't figure out she said.

"I want to go home." Finally, she spoke clearly enough to be understood. "I want to see Shade tomorrow." In a very, as her mother would say, unladylike manner, she wiped her nose with the back of her hand.

"We'll go home tomorrow," Mikayla said and the video ended with Jenessa crying on her shoulder.

Handing the phone back to her, she still couldn't

remember that particular part, but it obviously happened.

"Do you love Shade?" Mikayla asked.

"Yes," Jenessa answered without even thinking. There had been no reason for her to hide it.

"Do you want him back?"

"Yes."

"Do you want to go home?"

"Yes."

The heaviness she continually felt on her chest seemed to be lifting. Slightly.

"Let's go home." Mikayla moved off the bed, and she followed.

Right now, she had only one thing on her mind. Getting back to Shade.

The plane seemed to take forever to get to Boston and the traffic to Manchester had been insane. But somehow, they made it. On the flight, Jenessa devised a plan to contact Shade as soon as she arrived home and have him come over. They would sit down, and she would lay it all out on the table.

Mikayla seemed to be overjoyed by the plan, even though it was terribly simple and not clearly thought out. Jenessa felt it should be more complex. Especially after the three years of shit he had gone through because of her. She even debated if she needed to give him some sort of gift when he came over. What do you get your husband whom you're separated from and treated like crap?

When they arrived at the house, it was early evening. The sun hadn't completely set. It just highlighted the sky with some of the most stunning colors. Even though Jenessa had a wave of nervousness around her, she knew this would get her and Shade back together. It probably wouldn't happen instantly. They had to rebuild it slowly.

Now, she was ready to do it. She wanted to make this work.

"Who's that?" Mikayla questioned turning the car into the driveway.

At the front door stood an average height male with thinning gray hair. He seemed to be a health nut by his body-builder physique. When she stepped out of the vehicle and shut the car door, he spun around from the noise.

"May I help you?" Jenessa inquired, walking up her driveway, with a deep curiosity about his presence on her front steps.

"Are you Jenessa Wooten?" He glanced at the large manila envelope in his hands.

"Yes," she answered.

"You've been served." He handed her the envelope and rushed away.

"What is it?" Mikayla was now by her side.

Ripping open the flap, she pulled out several papers stapled together. Reading the title her heart dropped and tears burned her eyes.

"What is it?" Mikayla questioned again.

Clearing away the lump of sadness choking her, she said, "Shade has filed for divorce."

CHAPTER ELEVEN
Shade

The Bears' crowd did the official growl as the countdown to the final buzzer began. When the sound rang through the air, the Bears had skated away with another win. The team congratulated each other as they moved off the ice and toward the locker room.

Shade sat in his stall, tugging off his jersey, pads, and skates. Even though he was thrilled about the win and moving closer to the top of the standings, his mind had been elsewhere.

According to his attorney, it had been a week since Jenessa had been served the divorce papers. Shade sat in the bathroom at Jarvis's condo and cried once he received the news. Mikayla had sent videos and pictures of her and Jenessa in Las Vegas. He didn't think she could get any more beautiful. He'd been wrong. He still had trouble knowing she just flew off to Las Vegas, but she deserved a break from her job. As he studied every photo on his phone, she never looked happier.

His leaving helped her, although it broke him.

"Shade." Cat's voice broke into his thoughts. "The media wants to speak with you first." She flashed her bright smile at him.

"Fine." He nodded keeping his tone even. Since coming back from Buffalo, Cat seemed to be everywhere he'd been. He did his best to keep it professional, but she'd definitely upped her flirting.

"Do you need any assistance?" She batted her eyes at him.

"No." He stood putting his back to her. He knew it was rude but didn't know what else to do to get his point across.

He moved out to the media center designed for them to be interviewed. Reporters surrounded him and began the barrage of questions. The Bears had seriously been the talk of the PHL since the beginning of the season and have continued to keep up the media momentum.

When he finished he went back into the locker room, showered, dressed, and left without hardly saying anything to anyone. In the truck, he didn't even turn on the radio. The silence was loud enough for him.

Walking into the condo he was greeted by the cold stare coming from Mikayla's glare. Since Jenessa had received the papers, she had stopped talking to him. Tonight, he ducked his head down and rushed to the spare room. Almost like a dog with his tail between his legs.

After hanging up his suit, he crawled into bed and tried his best to fall asleep. It had grown harder and harder for him to have a restful night.

All because he missed his wife.

Shade strolled into the arena and felt a bit weird since there weren't many people around. This morning he had to do some promo bits for the Bears' social media. As captain, he was the unofficial face of the Bears' team. This was all new to him. Yes, he had known this part would be a bigger role than he'd been a part of before. However, today he didn't want to be here.

His shoulders deflated when he saw Cat talking to the cameraman. His lack of sleep had not prepared him for dealing with her today.

"Morning, Shade." She bounced over to him.

Her low-cut shirt hadn't gone unnoticed, even though he adverted his eyes. He had no desire to do anything with her or to her. Jenessa held his heart and forever will.

"Hey," he mumbled moving over to the table where the new Bear's merchandise laid. "Where am I starting?"

"Oh, you can start anywhere you'd like." She cooed, moving closer to him.

Instantly, he moved away from her, feeling uncomfortable. "Which shirt, Cat?" he questioned firmly.

"This one." She picked it up and laid it on her chest. "Do you need any assistance?" She gave him a sly smirk.

"No." He picked up another shirt off the table. "We'll start here."

"I'm here to *assist* you," she continued, unfazed by his abrupt answers.

"I'm fine." He turned and began to rush away.

"You can change here," she said.

He didn't give her a response as he left to go to a nearby bathroom. He was going to have to talk with Kian about Cat. He didn't want to be around her anymore. She truly was making him uncomfortable.

When he came back out, he avoided eye contact with her at all costs. He only listened to the direction of the cameraman. When Cat put in her opinion, he would only do it if he felt like it and never commented on anything she said.

After four more changes and what seemed to be ten thousand photos, the photo shoot was complete. Again, Shade hurried to get back into his original shirt and tried to leave before she could corner him. Somehow he managed to get out of the arena and into his truck. Checking the time, he knew there wouldn't be any point going to the condo since practice started soon. Instead, he drove over to The Latte Bean to grab a flavored water.

He easily found a place to park, went in and ordered. He was pleased to find an empty table in the back. Staring out the window, he watched the people walk past. The weather slowly had begun to cool, which proved the holiday season would be upon quickly. This brought even more pain to his heart. It would be the first time in ten years he wouldn't spend it with Jenessa. Prior to meeting her, the holidays didn't mean much to him. Occasionally, he'd receive a gift but nothing of real value.

Until her.

Their first Christmas hadn't been too long after they met. Even though they wouldn't be together on the actual day of Christmas, they decided to celebrate the weekend before. Shade had to practice while on break but would spend every possible moment with her. Obviously, Jenessa told him not to get her anything. However, he wanted to give her the best gift he could think of. In between classes, practice, and games, he managed to pick up a few additional shifts at a restaurant as a dishwasher. They paid him cash, which Shade knew was wrong since he wouldn't pay taxes on it. However, it wasn't a large sum of money. Just enough to help with day to day expenses.

He went to a secondhand store and managed to find some Christmas decorations. Then he went to purchase a small tree. He took the rest of his money and rented a cheap motel room and ordered her favorite takeout. It took him all day to put up everything in the room. He knew it wasn't high-end or fancy, he just hoped she would like it. Looking at the one gift under the teeny tree, it made him smile.

She'd love it.

Laying out the take-out food on the paper plates on the small table, a knock came to the door. Shade became slightly nervous as he opened the door. On the other side, Jenessa stood with a bright smile and a Christmas bag in one hand.

"What are we doing here?" she asked with a giggle.

"Close your eyes," he said.

She did.

He took her unoccupied hand and led her into the room. Guiding her into the center of it, he left her side for a brief second to shut off the light.

Coming back to her side, he said, "Open them."

Jenessa's mouth dropped as she slowly turned around, studying every part of the room. "This is beautiful, Shade. I love all of this."

"I know it's not much." He shrugged, even though pleased with himself on being able to accomplish it all.

She gently kissed his lips. "It's perfect.

"How about we eat?" he suggested.

"I do believe I smell my favorite fried rice." She giggled again. "Oh, I'll put this under our tree."

'Our tree'. The two words made his heart race with elation.

They went over to the table with only one chair. He planned to sit on the bed, but Jenessa picked up both plates and went over to the bed. Shade grabbed the drinks and followed her. As they ate, they discussed their day, hockey, and the upcoming semester. Shade always enjoyed the ease they had to converse with each other.

When they finished with the food, he moved everything off the bed.

"Do we get to open presents now?" Jenessa gleefully asked.

"Sure." Shade tried to hide the apprehension in his voice. He knew his gift was not going to be anything spectacular. She'd probably think it was a dumb idea. Picking up the rectangular box he handed it to her.

Ripping the paper away in a flash and opening the flimsy box, Jenessa gasped. Shade's cheeks burned because he couldn't tell if it was a good or bad gasp.

"You gave me your favorite hoodie." She beamed, pulling out the navy blue hoodie with the word 'State' across the front. "I've been trying to figure out a way to steal this from you." She laughed, hugging the hoodie to her chest.

He smiled. "You always said it has a lot of great memories."

"I love it." She leaned over and kissed him. "Your turn." She rushed over to get the Christmas bag and handed it to him.

Inside was a much larger rectangular box. When he pulled it out, he inspected it first. The plain white box had no special design, but it felt expensive. Much better than the cheap one he gave her.

"Open it up, Shade," Jenessa said, practically bouncing next to him on the bed.

Carefully, he removed the lid. Red tissue paper covered whatever was hidden inside. Pulling back the paper, he froze.

"Tada," she exclaimed. "What do you think?"

Shade had no words as he stared down at the highly expensive black leather winter coat. A winter coat. His fingertips softly touched the cool material. He instantly moved it away, afraid he'd mark the perfectly untouched leather.

"What's wrong?" Jenessa's enthusiasm left.

"This had to cost you a lot," he managed to say.

"Well, no…not really," she stammered over her words. "If you want to know the truth, it was on sale."

He remained silent.

"Hey." Jenessa's concerned tone matched her touch as she placed her hand on his upper back. "What's wrong?"

Suddenly feeling embarrassed, he stood up and set the box to the side. Normally, he never let his emotions go out of whack. However, they were all over the place right now.

"Shade," she said his name more firmly.

He leaned against the wall.

"Talk to me, please." She moved closer to him.

Crossing his arms, he hung his head.

"Don't shut me out, Shade," she begged, putting her hands on his crossed forearms.

"My gift wasn't as good as yours," he confessed. Saying the words left a bad taste in his mouth.

"This is the best Christmas I've ever had," she admitted.

Shade shook his head. "The tree should be bigger. All the lights should match. We should be in a hotel in a better neighborhood. I should have gotten you jewelry." He ticked off all the reasons in his head as he said them out loud.

"This is an incredible night. You put so much thought and love into all of this. It's much more than I could ever imagine." She moved her hands to cup his face, forcing him to look at her. "I got you a winter coat because the one you have is thinner than a bedsheet. I love you, and I don't want you to freeze to death. If I knew your shoe size,

I would have gotten you boots too. You run around in gym shoes and there's two feet of snow outside."

He glanced at his coat hanging on the hook near the door. He's had it for over five years. The jacket was too big, and the lining had been worn away from the previous owner.

"You deserve better."

"I deserve you." Jenessa kissed his lips.

At that moment, Shade truly felt at home and truly loved.

"You look like someone just kicked your puppy."

The memory had been startled away by Mikayla's voice.

His reality came back. He sat in The Latte Bean with lemon and lime infused water in front of him. Untouched. The world had continued to move around him as he sat there.

"I figured you were still giving me the silent treatment," he said.

Mikayla took a seat across from him. "You're still an asshole for filing those papers."

Since she'd returned from Las Vegas, Mikayla had given him nothing but glares.

"Jarvis is an asshole but you speak to him." He tried to joke with her.

"I've trained him a bit to be less of one," she commented.

Shade smirked because Jarvis had grown up a lot since they'd gotten together.

"Why did you do it, Shade?" Hurt filled the question.

"For her happiness," he told her truthfully.

"She'd be happy with you," she offered.

"I saw the photos, Kay. She was glowing. Do you know what the difference is? Me. I'm not in the picture." He picked up the cup to take a sip but put it down. Nothing seemed to appeal to him right now.

"Men are so dense." Mikayla rolled her eyes.

"Why?" he inquired.

Glaring at him she said, "You know Nes as much as I do. Has she just picked up and hopped on a plane to go somewhere? Has she ever gone on a vacation without a PowerPoint, PDF, and an itinerary of every single minute planned out? Does *that* sound like the happy, go-get 'em Jenessa you know?"

He admitted it didn't sound like her at all. Anytime—well, every time—Jenessa planned a trip, she'd plan every part of it. She would even print out descriptions of landmarks she'd want to visit and read it to Shade as they traveled to the destination. He didn't care as long as they were spending time together, and she was happy.

"I'm begging you, Shade. *Begging.* Please talk to her before anything else is filed. Just sit and talk."

He noticed the wetness in her eyes from the now forming tears.

"You two are meant to be together. You know this better than anyone. She needs you and you need her." Mikayla stood. "It's time for you to man up or regret it for the rest of your life."

With those words, she left him sitting alone at the table.

Practice started out smoothly, except Shade didn't want to be there. Hockey was all he had left, and he'd rather be anywhere else. He stood with the rest of the team, listening to Hamilton's strategy for the game tomorrow night. As they broke into squads, he noticed Cat was sitting in the stands with a few of the front office employees. She stared directly at him, and he knew he'd have to do something about it and soon. He had enough going on he didn't need her trouble.

Thankfully, practice did distract him from the world outside. Nonetheless, when it finished it all came rushing back to him. Inside the locker room, Edgar invited him to lunch with a bunch of the other guys. Food sounded good, and he agreed to go.

As they all made their way to the best sub shop in town, Shade wondered if he would run into Jenessa. This was her favorite spot to eat. Walking in, he glanced around almost hoping to see if she was eating there. He didn't so he shuffled up to the counter. He ordered and watched them create his sub and hand it to him. He sat at the end of the large corner booth where Jarvis, Edgar, Zerrick, and Jackson were already seated.

Their conversation rolled between upcoming games, certain players, and the holidays. Janan and Nova sent out an email lining out the events. Shade knew he would need to attend them all because of his position on the team. Trying to see the positive side of it all, at least he wouldn't be alone for the majority of the holidays.

"You seem to be lost in thought," Edgar leaned over and said while everyone at the table stared at him.

"Sort of," he mumbled, not really wanting to get into it.

"What's going on?" Edgar asked.

"He filed his divorce papers," Jarvis announced.

All at once, everyone began to talk. Each one pretty much saying what he felt. An idiot.

"Thanks." He shot the look of death at his friend.

"Why would you do it?" Edgar questioned in complete shock.

"No point in putting off the inevitable." Shade took a small bite of his sub.

"How many concussions have you had?" Edgar continued his inquiry.

"A couple. Why?" He furrowed his brow at this line of questioning.

"I'm trying to figure out why you're a moron." His seriousness made the table chuckle. Although, Shade hadn't found it funny. He knew Edgar well enough to know his comment was no laughing matter.

"What else was I supposed to do?" he countered.

"Have you talked to her?" He shot back, causing the table to grow quiet.

"No."

"Then you are a moron."

Glancing around the table the guys did their best to avoid his stares or give him a sad smile. Feeling like shit, Shade scooted himself out of the booth and left the sub shop.

Jumping in his truck, he didn't know where to go or do. He thought about going to the condo but being cooped up in there sounded displeasing. His body felt too tired for a run, but his stomach rumbled. He hadn't finished his food and was still hungry.

Driving to the grocery store, everything seemed to be weighing on him. Maybe he should have reached out to Jenessa. Just one more time. Would it have made a difference? He tried many, many times to get her to see and understand he had been trying to help her. He used all his strength to keep them together. He gave her space then tried to pull her back to him, and she shut him down. Time after time.

When the first year passed, he almost thought they would be on the mend. He was wrong. Jenessa began picking up more and more cases, keeping her in the office longer. He planned several getaways and vacations, but they were all canceled. She could never go for one reason or another.

As the second year came and went Shade craved her touch. He hinted around to them being intimate or even hugging, but a cold shoulder had been all he received. Sure, he masturbated in the shower, like some teenager, but his fantasies were always of her.

This past year was when he stopped communicating with her. Only short sentences and nods. He even began sleeping in the den. What point was it to sleep in their bed? Nothing happened there or even on the sectional.

Strolling into the store, he picked up a basket and aimlessly went through the aisles. He searched through the produce, grabbing some fruit and vegetables. He ended up in the junk food section as Jenessa called it. Even though they both loved this particular section, they tried to avoid it. Today he craved it all. Dropping a couple of bags of chips into the basket, he walked a bit further down to figure out which dip he wanted.

"You know this is all bad for you."

Shade froze. It took him a couple of seconds to turn and see Jenessa standing behind him.

"Hey," he breathed out his greeting.

"Hi." She gave him a small smile. "You should get the cheese dip for the corn chips."

"Huh?"

Jenessa pointed at his basket and he had completely forgotten where he was or what he was doing.

"Right. Sure. Yes," he blurted out the words he thought made sense.

An awkward silence fell between them. He only stared at her. Her long hair was down, resting on her back and shoulders. She wore a thin workout hoodie and leggings. He figured she went to yoga. This pleased him because it meant she was doing something she enjoyed.

"Um…congratulations on being named captain," she finally said.

"Thanks. Not sure what everyone was thinking picking me." He didn't mean to say the last part. But he never kept his feelings from her.

"They were thinking you're the best person for the job."

Shade shrugged, overcome by emotions from her compliment. This had been the most they've spoken to each other without arguing in…he couldn't remember how long.

"What are you making?" he asked glancing in her basket. He wanted to continue talking to her and not leave.

"Mikayla has eaten all the macaroni and cheese. So, I needed to restock." She sighed.

Chuckling, he understood. Mikayla ate the stuff as fast

as Kraft made it.

"I still suck at cooking," she added. "So, there's not much in here."

"You're still learning." Shade hated to say she *was* a horrible cook. It just wasn't a strong suit for her.

"I try." He wanted to say a thousand things to her. All of which sat on the tip of his tongue.

"Well…um…see ya." Jenessa was the first to walk away.

"See ya," he repeated while watching her back.

When she was only a few feet away, she looked back. Their eyes locked, both talking silently, begging for the other to say what laid on their hearts and chests. Shade wanted to kiss her, hold her, tell her how much he missed and loved her.

Instead, they both turned and walked away.

Unsure of what he was doing or where he was going, Shade ended up knocking on Edgar's door. When he answered, he scanned Shade up and down.

"You look like shit," Edgar said after completing his observation.

"I feel like it too," Shade confessed.

"Come on in." He stepped to the side, inviting him into his home.

"Am I interrupting anything?" Shade didn't want to intrude on any of his family time.

"My wife is out conquering the world, and my children are…well, being teenagers who don't need their father unless it involves money," Edgar said then led the way to the kitchen. Shade took a seat as Edgar grabbed a couple of glasses of water.

"So, what's going on?"

Taking a sip, the water cooled his throat. Shade began

telling him what happened at the grocery store.

"And you walked away?" Edgar asked.

"I did."

"You're an idiot." He sighed and shook his head.

"I know." Shade couldn't argue with him. He had an opportunity to speak with her and blew it. Regret filled every cell in his body. "How am I going to fix this?"

"You know how," Edgar firmly told him. "Call her. Go to her. Fucking talk to her."

"I already filed the papers. She'll never forgive me." Hanging his head, he was ready to kick his own ass for letting the attorney file them.

"Personally, I believe she will. However, you'll never know until you *talk* to her." He kept the same tone.

"I just want everything to go back to normal." Shade's begging tone hadn't been for Edgar but for the universe to hear his plea.

"There's nothing normal about marriage. Every day is different. Some days are challenging. Some days are smooth as silk. But the best part is being by the side of your best friend every single day."

Lifting his head, Shade saw Edgar hadn't just been talking about him and Jenessa, but about himself and Greer. He knew they had been together for almost twenty years. Their marriage was one all the players were jealous of. They had a perfect marriage.

"Don't wait, Shade. Go."

As much as his entire body wanted to run to her, he didn't move. Yes, he loved her. Yes, they belonged together, but a small part was still hurt by all the pain she caused him the past three years. Knowing he should move past it, he couldn't for some reason. Their love had grown to something different now. Something painful.

CHAPTER TWELVE
Jenessa

During the last part of the yoga class, Jenessa didn't feel any relaxation. In fact, she didn't even want to be there. Since seeing Shade yesterday at the grocery store, she had only been thinking about everything she should have told him.

"Hey."

Jenessa opened her eyes and saw Greer smiling down at her.

"Class is over."

"Oh." She sat up, realizing almost everyone had left. Only a few stragglers remained.

"Want to hit the juice bar?" Greer suggested with a hopeful smile.

Jenessa had the urge to say no and hide away in her home, but something told her to go. After gathering up her items, they strolled over and placed their order. When they got their drinks, Greer led the way to the table.

"You look miserable. Do you want to talk about it?" Greer's motherly tone was soothing to her.

She hadn't even told Mikayla about seeing Shade at the store. She still couldn't process everything herself. However, she knew Greer would listen without judgment.

Taking a deep breath, she told her all about Las Vegas and her plan on talking to Shade. She also told her about being served with the divorce papers. Leaving out her feelings in the tale, she then went on to tell her about seeing him at the store and their short, awkward conversation.

When she finished, Greer didn't say anything. According to her expression of disbelief, she probably didn't know what to say.

"Let's take a step back," she finally spoke. "Why did you run off to Vegas? I know you well enough to know it's not in your wheelhouse to jump up and leave town."

"Truthfully, I needed to get away from Manchester. I felt as if I was being strangled." For the first time, she said what she'd been hiding deep within her.

"I understand that statement more than you think." Greer flashed her a small smile.

"Being away I did manage to figure out a lot. Not every detail, but I knew we needed to sit down and talk." She failed at hiding the emotion in her tone.

"Then you came home and were hit with the papers," she confirmed.

"Yes."

"And what happened then?"

Jenessa paused, unsure how deep she *should* be with Greer. Even though they're friends, she was still married to Edgar, who was one of Shade's best friends.

"I'm certain you were shocked," Greer continued.

"Not as much as you think." Jenessa decided to let it all go. "I deserved it. He should have left me a long time ago."

"No, Jenessa." Greer placed her hand over hers. "You both went through something no parent should ever have to go through. It's every parent's worst nightmare. But you two can get over this hurdle. You both need to sit down and talk. There will be tears, maybe some arguing. However, when all the smoke settles, your love will hold you together."

Greer's words spun around her. They touched every part of her heart and soul. In Las Vegas, she tried to run away from all her problems and emotions. Everything she'd been hiding and never believing it truly was there. The only conclusion she officially came to—she wanted Shade. She needed to apologize, tell him she made a massive mistake in the way she treated him and start over.

How do they start over?

"I'm a failure, Greer." The words left her as the tears filled her eyes.

"Why do you say you're a failure?"

"I let him down. I killed our son. I shut everyone out. I ruined our marriage." Tears slowly rolled down her cheeks.

"Jenessa Wooten!" Greer gasped. "You didn't kill your son. As a mother, I completely understand where you're coming from. We're meant to protect our babies at any and every cost. It's our one job. It never ever goes away. However, your beautiful baby didn't die because of you. *You* did everything right."

Jenessa tried her best to swallow the lump forming in her throat. She couldn't do it. Instead, covering her mouth, she tried to fight the emotions that were about to erupt. She wasn't strong enough this time. Greer pulled her chair around to hers and wrapped her up in a hug.

They remained holding each other until Jenessa calmed down. Greer handed her several napkins to clean her face.

"I must look like an idiot," she mumbled, wiping her cheeks and nose.

"No. You look like a wife and mother who's hurting," Greer corrected her.

"I'm a mess." Jenessa managed to compose herself. Somewhat. Greer wouldn't release her hold.

"Yes. A fixable mess."

"Greer, he'll never forgive me." She sniffled, dabbing her eyes again. "I wouldn't forgive me if I were in his shoes."

"You have to stop thinking this way. Shade loves you.

He wouldn't have stayed as long as he had if he didn't want anything to do with you."

By her tone, it left no point in arguing with her.

"You know what to do," Greer told her. "You need to go to him."

"What if—"

"No." She cut her off. "There's no *what if*. You can't fight your pain anymore. You need to heal. You and Shade both need to heal. Together." Her motherly tone was long gone. Now the words were a clear command.

Taking two deep breaths something happened. The emotions balanced themselves out. A wave of confidence came over her. A strength she hadn't truly felt in the longest time. She had to fight for her and Shade. No matter what. They were meant to be together.

Period.

"I have to find Shade." She finally glanced over at Greer.

"Practice is about to finish. Go to the arena."

Before she could say anything else, Jenessa grabbed her yoga bag and rushed out the door.

She couldn't remember how she arrived so fast at the arena. Walking up to the security guard, she worried her name wouldn't be on the access list. However, she gave him her name, and he opened the door.

Jenessa tried to remember the last time she'd been in this part of the arena. Maybe Christmas last year. She'd attempted to come to a Bears' family event, only to run out before it started and anyone could see her. Now, she strolled the lengthy hall. In her mind, she tried to figure out what she'd say to him. Would he walk away? It could be a real possibility.

As she got closer to the locker room, she could hear voices. Knowing she couldn't go into the locker room, she slowed her pace and stopped about fifty yards from the double doors.

A few moments, later she began seeing the players

coming out of the tunnel. Moving back, she slightly hid around the corner and peeked around it. There was no rhyme or reason why she suddenly acted like a spy.

Then she saw him.

Shade.

He stood with his back to her, obviously not noticing her lurking skills.

"Who are we staring at?"

Jenessa jumped a foot into the air and loudly gasped. "What the hell, Edgar?" She slapped his shoulder.

He chuckled. "Greer told me you were coming."

"Well did she ask you to scare me to death?" She clutched her chest, hoping to stall her racing heart.

"Nah. That was a perk for me." He grinned. "Why are you hiding like a stalker?"

"I'm not sure he wants to see me." She figured Greer already told him everything about their conversation.

"He loves you and has been miserable since he left you. Trust me, he wants to talk to you and be with you." Edgar, like Greer, had a tone to his voice which made you feel safe and loved, even when scolding you.

"I don't want to bother him, but could you tell him I'll wait by the truck." She gave him a small smile.

"I'll tell him right away." He grinned again.

She thanked him and made her way back up the hall and out the door, without being seen. Shade's truck was easy to spot. The players' cars in the parking lot were always the newest vehicle. Shade had a 2004 Chevy Silverado. She dropped the tailgate and hopped down on it to sit. Remembering numerous discussions between them about upgrading the truck but he said there was nothing wrong with it. Meaning he won't get another one until the wheels fell off.

She sat there for several minutes doing nothing more than swinging her legs. She didn't know how much time passed, but it couldn't have been much since Shade came rushing out to her.

"Are you okay?" he asked, almost out of breath when he reached her.

"Did you come straight from the shower?" Water was dripping onto his face from his drenched hair. His shirt stuck to his chest and arms.

"Sort of. Edgar told me you were waiting for me."

His actions of getting to her so quickly made her heart beat a little faster. "I didn't want to bother you."

"You don't, and you know you can *bother* me anytime and anywhere," he spoke softly as if he didn't know how she would respond to his words.

"I just wanted to ask if you would like to have dinner with me." Nervousness came over her. Although she shouldn't be with Shade.

"When? Where?"

Hearing the excitement in his voice made her calm. "If you're available tonight, we can eat at the house," she suggested.

"I can't wait." Again, he kept the same elated tone.

"Okay. I'll see you at six?" She hopped off from the tailgate.

"Great. Yes. Sure." He hurried out his words.

"I'll see you then." She gave him a small smile before leaving to move toward her car. She tried to not look back but was unable to resist. Just as she thought, he was staring at her.

When she reached her car, the nervousness quickly turned to panic. She couldn't cook and didn't know what to order. Then she wondered what she should wear, or what to do with her hair. Every tiny detail spun her deeper into this panic. Something she never ever did. Pulling out her phone, she called Mikayla.

"What's up, sis?"

"Can you meet me at the sub shop? I need your help." She couldn't be sure she even breathed in between words.

"What's wrong?" Mikayla questioned.

"I just left Shade at the arena and asked him to dinner."

"I'll be there in ten minutes." She squealed and ended the call.

Jenessa ordered food for them both and waited patiently in a booth for Mikayla. She said ten minutes, but it was closer to thirty when she strolled into the place.

"First, I'm starving." She slid into the booth. "Second, tell me everything."

They unwrapped their subs as Jenessa began to tell her about yoga class, her breakdown and breakthrough with Greer, talking to Edgar, and asking Shade to dinner.

"You can't even imagine my happiness level at this moment." Mikayla beamed.

"I'm a wreck." She glanced down at her untouched sub.

"Why?" Her bright smile turned into a frown.

"Oh, jeesh let me see." She rolled her eyes. "I just asked my husband, who left me and filed for divorce, to come have dinner with me. I can't cook, so I guess we'll have peanut butter and jelly sandwiches. I have no idea what to wear. Should it be casual? Sexy? Something in-between? Should I just blurt out how I'm feeling? Or should I apologize first? Will he run in the other direction? Will he forgive me? Should he forgive me?" She had to stop and breathe. All the questions, concerns, and feelings continued to spin around her like a tornado.

"Okay, that's a lot to process in twenty seconds." She appeared to be winded as well.

"Well…" Jenessa shrugged unable to say anything else because it was a lot for her.

"Let's start from the beginning," Mikayla said. "Yes, you and Shade are on a bit of a…hiatus, which I personally believe is a temporary situation. Secondly, everyone knows you're a horrifically, horrible cook. Especially Shade because the poor guy has eaten your food for years. I'm still not sure how he's never had food poisoning."

Jenessa crossed her arms and glared at her. "You're being a *bit* dramatic."

"Trust me. I'm not," she countered. "Thirdly, wear something you're comfortable in. You don't need to be fancy with Shade. He doesn't do fancy."

She couldn't argue with her there. Shade would always be a jeans and a T-shirt kind of guy.

"Lastly, neither of you have ever had trouble talking to each other. Just say what you want to him. He'll never run away from you."

As much as she wanted that to be true, she couldn't be sure now. So much had happened between them. A lot of hurt, sadness, and much of it would never be forgiven. No matter what Mikayla said.

"Just talk."

Two words everyone kept telling her to do, and now she had to do it.

Jenessa sat at the edge of either screaming, crying, or pulling out her hair. Possibly all three at the same time. Why did she think she could cook? Right now, she was trying to figure out why the noodles are clumped into one big brick. The sauce, which should be bright red, now looked black and smelled worse than it looked.

The doorbell rang, which caused Jenessa to throw everything down onto the counter and run to the door. Opening it, Shade stood on the other side. He wore a pair of dark jeans and a light blue polo with his leather jacket. The same jacket she bought him for their first Christmas many, many years ago.

"Hi," he greeted her with a turned-up nose. "Are you cooking?"

Before she could answer, the smoke alarm went off. "Dammit," she yelled.

Together they both rushed to the kitchen. Smoke rolled out of the oven as Shade opened it. Grabbing a towel, he jerked out the completely black bricks of what should have been garlic bread. She had forgotten she had put them in the oven.

"Fuck! Fuck! Fuck!" she yelled at the smoke detector as she used another towel to fan the smoke.

Shade dumped everything into the sink and opened the window, helping to air it out.

"Jen, this is burnt," he commented while moving the pan off the burner and turning it off.

"Fuck!" She threw the towel across the room, and the smoke alarm finally stopped screeching.

"It's okay," he said calmly.

"I was trying to make something nice," she grumbled. "I'm just the worst cook."

"You're still learning." He smiled.

His words, like always, seemed to bring a calm to her. He never would say how awful she truly was as a cook. Only encouraged her.

"I can get us something from Grub Hub," he suggested.

"Yeah. Sounds good."

He tapped on his phone, and she poured each of them a glass of water and carried them into the den. She knew they needed some fresher air as the kitchen still had smoke lingering in the air.

Once she settled into the sectional, her nerves began to take over when he walked in. Shrugging off his jacket, he laid it on the other end of the sectional and came over to her. When she handed him the glass, her hands lightly shook.

"Thanks." He took a small sip and set the glass on the table.

Taking a big gulp from her glass, she then placed it

next to his. Remembering Mikayla's words, she knew this was Shade, and she didn't have to be nervous around him.

"How was practice?" she asked, keeping her tone even.

"Not bad."

"Season seems to be going great."

"Yes. We are looking up. Glad we're not at the bottom."

They had been through the Bears being in last place and fighting to be recognized. Now they were in the top ten of the league.

For several seconds, they just sat awkwardly next to each other in silence.

"How have you been?" he asked in a soft tone.

As she opened her mouth to automatically say fine, she stopped. She was far from fine.

"How have you been?" She returned his question with the same question.

He sighed. "Honestly, I don't know."

"Same here."

Again, silence filled the room. She could hear every hum and creak in the whole house. However, Greer, Mikayla, and even Edgar's voices were yelling in her head to talk.

"I can't explain how I'm doing because it's hard to put everything into words," she started.

"You can try," he urged with a hopeful expression.

She stared into his sad brown eyes. She craved to know everything and anything he felt. The burn of tears quickly crept up. For so long, she'd pushed him away. She owed him this. Of course, when she opened her mouth to say something, the doorbell rang.

"I'll get it." He stood and left the room.

Her shoulders sagged. She'd been so tense with nervousness and every other emotion in the book, she wondered how much more her body could take. When he walked back in with a large pizza box and then opened it her heart sank.

"Shade, you didn't have to get pepperoni pizza. I know you hate it."

He had told her the story about him eating out of a dumpster, and since then he very, very rarely ate pizza, especially pepperoni.

"I know you like it." He placed a piece on a paper plate, handing it to her.

Even during all of this, he still put her feelings before his. With her stomach in knots, she couldn't eat. Putting the plate down she turned her body toward him.

"I don't know where to begin," she said.

Keeping himself facing forward, he placed his elbows on his knees. "Starting from the beginning is always good."

Taking a deep breath, she knew he was right. "I have done a lot of things wrong in my life. Number one is being a bitch to you. I can't explain all the pain I felt. I could never process it, and I'm not sure I'm doing it very well right now.

She stared at Shade's profile, trying to gauge his reaction. There was none.

"I pushed you away because I can't find any happiness in me. I can't remember how to laugh, or smile, or...even love." She paused, watching Shade drop his head.

"I don't think you'll ever forgive me. For three years, I've caused you pain. All because of my pain. You know me well enough to know I don't deal well with my emotions. It's why we made such a great team because you always knew how to keep me level."

Shade's head remained down.

"We make a great team because..." She swallowed the growing lump in her throat. She had to say it. She couldn't take it any longer. "We're soul mates. We always love each other. I'm not sure you'll ever forgive me or give me a second chance, but I hope so."

Tears streamed down her face, but Shade gave no reaction.

"Mikayla told me she heard you crying, and it breaks

my heart you couldn't rely on me." She told me the truth. "We should have been healing together. Instead, I put a wall up to close you out."

He sat up and looked at her. His eyes were wet. "You didn't think I could be emotional over our son's death?"

"I've never seen you cry." As soon as the words left, she knew they sounded ridiculous.

"Jen, I may not cry at the end of a romance movie, but you know I'm not ice cold." His tone clearly stated how hurt he'd been by her statement, but the pain was in his eyes.

"I apologize." Now, she hung her head. "This isn't going the way I thought."

"How do you want it to go?" he questioned.

Lifting her head, their eyes connected. This would be her one chance to tell him. Tell him what she craved. "I hope you will forgive me and give me a second chance."

They remained locked in their positions until Shade made a move.

"I'm going to head out." He rose from the sectional.

"What?" Jenessa gasped as she followed him all the way to the front door.

Then he stopped and faced her.

"Give me some time."

His words tore at her. She knew it wouldn't happen overnight or instantaneously but never imagined he would leave.

"Okay." She didn't know where the sob came from, but it did.

Suddenly, his large arms wrapped around her pulling her close. Clinging to his chest and shirt, she cried. Once she calmed herself a bit, she felt his lips on her temple.

"I have a road game tomorrow. When I come back, we'll talk more. I promise." He kissed her cheek this time before releasing her and walking out the door.

Jenessa wiped her face and went back into the den. There, she saw his leather coat sitting on the other end of the sectional. Slipping her arms into it, she held it close to herself and inhaled Shade's scent. He still never wore anything powerful. Always soft and minty. Laying on the cushions, she continued to cry until she closed her eyes.

CHAPTER THIRTEEN
Shade

The plane ride back from the road game had been exhausting for Shade in more ways than one. His focus should have been on the game they lost and for it not to happen again. Instead, his mind was only focused on one thing. Or in this case person.

Jenessa.

Her words from yesterday should have made him elated. However, it scared him. The second chance they both wanted was in his grasp, but suddenly fear came over him heavier than the happiness. Could his heart take any more pain?

"You've been staring out that window as if you're trying to solve the universe's problems," Edgar startled him.

"Something like it." He turned to his seatmate.

"Jenessa?"

"Yeah." He sighed. "We talked. Well, she talked. I listened."

"And? Are you back together?" he asked with a nosy, happy tone.

"No."

"What? Why?" he asked, completely surprised by his

answer.

"I can't explain it."

"Sure you can," Edgar pushed. "It might even help you."

"It'll only sound stupid if I say it out loud," Shade said.

"Try me."

He thought of a hundred ways to say what he felt, but there was only one real way.

"I'm afraid I won't be able to handle any more heartache." He managed to keep his words low, not wanting the others on the plane to hear him. Although most of them were asleep.

"I understand. There's nothing more painful than having the one you love the most cause said pain. To this day, I'm not sure how you went this long without losing your mind."

Shade listened intently to his words.

"My mother always said God only gives you what you can handle."

This statement made him furrow his brow. "When did you become religious?"

"I *said* my mother would say it. But it's true. You need to try because you'll regret it if you don't. That'll cause you more harm. If you go back and feel the same pain, then leave and hold your head up knowing you did the best you could."

Shade couldn't even attempt to argue with him. He was right. Yes, she might push him away again. Yes, the divorce might go through. However, he did want to try.

And he would.

When the alarm went off in the morning, Shade did not want to get out of his bed and go into practice. Tossing and turning throughout the night caused him not to get any rest.

Once he got to the arena, he felt a bit more awake. Only thanks to a breakfast sandwich and some orange juice. Changing and getting onto the ice, he forced himself to stay focused on Hamilton and the coaching staff. Somehow he managed to do just that all the way through practice.

As they made their way off the ice, Cat waited for him at the end of the tunnel. Shade groaned and rolled his eyes when he saw her standing there. This was the last person he wanted to deal with right now.

"Hi, Shade." She waved her fingers at him.

"Cat," he said her name with a deadpan tone.

"Oh." She pouted her lips. "Is someone tired?"

"What do you need, Cat?" He began to grow irate from her fake baby voice.

She opened her mouth but stopped when Edgar stepped up to Shade.

"Hey, Cat. How are you?" he asked in an overly cheerful voice.

"I'm good." She smiled. "I was just about to prep Shade for some new promos."

"Great, I'll come along," Edgar suggested.

"Oh, there's no need." Cat waved her hand. "It's only for Shade."

"I'm sure Kian won't mind my tagging along. I need to brush up on my acting skills." He chuckled.

"It's just for Shade." Her cheeks grew red.

"Why?" Shade finally asked after watching their interactions.

"Yea, why?" Edgar added.

Cat stammered a bit and was unable to complete any words.

"Is it because you want to get Shade alone?" Edgar called her out.

Suddenly, her whole appearance changed. "I don't think it's any of *your* business."

"It's *my* business." Shade grew angry at her demeanor. "Leave me alone, Cat. I don't want you around me anymore."

Cat's mouth dropped. Before anything else could be said Edgar tugged on his practice jersey, and together they turned and left her.

"You need to go to Cabel about her," Edgar told him when they were in the locker room.

"I am."

They changed, and Shade headed to the condo. He knew they had a game tonight, and he should rest, but he had a promise to keep. Once he got into his jogging clothes, he called Jenessa.

"Hello," she answered on the second ring.

"Want to go for a jog?" He omitted any greeting.

"Same place?" She didn't seem fazed by his omission.

"Yes."

"See you in ten minutes."

"Okay." He ended the call and headed to the park.

When he pulled into the parking lot, he immediately saw her car and parked next to it. Before Jenessa became pregnant they ran together at least a few times a week. He strolled over to the bench they always met at.

She didn't see him right away as she faced the other direction. He watched her for a few seconds. She tied her hair into a 'bird's nest' as he called it. She had on a pink hoodie and tight black workout pants. Her gym shoes matched her hoodie. He knew she took pride in her appearance and he'd been the opposite. As long as his clothes were clean and didn't have any holes, he was good.

"Hey." He approached her.

When she turned, a small smile appeared. "I didn't hear you come up."

"I just got here." He sat next to her.

"Rough day?" She turned to face him.

"A loss will do it," he commented.

"It's something else." She knew him well enough.

"A lot of things," he mumbled.

"We used to talk."

Glancing over at her, she silently begged him to talk. Her face said it all.

"We did." He nodded.

"We still can."

He cleared his throat. "I never thought we would be here."

"Me either."

They sat silently for several seconds before Shade realized how silly he'd been. This was *his* Jenessa. The woman of his dreams. His soul mate. There had been a lot of hurt, but here they were, giving it a chance.

"When I imagined our life together being divorced never ever came up," she started.

Shade mirrored her position on the bench. "Jen, you've hurt me in a way I can't put into words."

She hung her head.

"I'm not saying this to upset you. I'm trying to make you see my point of view."

Lifting her head, he saw the tears filling her eyes.

"I did everything I could do to show you how much I love you, how much I wanted to take away your pain, and I couldn't do enough." Shade spoke of his feelings he'd kept hidden for so long.

"There's no way for me to tell you how sorry I am, but you have to know the pain consumed me. I didn't know how to handle any of it."

"Neither did I. I lost my son too, Jen," he snapped then immediately regretted it. "I'm sorry."

"You have every right to be upset. For three years, I've treated you as if you're no one, and I hope you can forgive me." A single tear escaped her eye.

He almost wrapped her up in his arms but stopped himself. If he held her now, he'd never let her go.

"When you left and all those trade rumors were going around, I figured if you left, you'd be happy. In truth, it broke my heart more and more not having you with me," she confessed.

"They weren't rumors," he corrected her.

"What?"

"I asked to be traded. The reason I did was because I thought you would be better without me."

He watched her jaw drop.

"My contract is only good for this season," he continued. "When Janan and Nova asked me to be captain turning them down seemed like the right thing to do. If I left Manchester, you could heal."

"I'm not okay without you."

Now, it was his turn for his jaw to drop. Her words pierced him.

"I have tried to pretend I'm some tough, don't care about anything female, but it's a lie. I rely on you more than I thought I did. You bring balance to me and all my craziness. I just can't remember a time in my life where I needed anyone more." She paused. "I hope I bring you some happiness as well."

"Jenessa, you know you're my life. You balance me out just as I do you. Maybe I should have told you all the pain I was in, instead of hiding it. I felt I needed to be strong for you."

Jenessa placed her hand on top of his. The warm touch made his heart race.

"You're strong, Shade. The strongest man I know."

Laying his other hand over hers, he gently rubbed the pad of his thumb over her knuckles.

"I'm sorry I hid behind my work. I should have communicated with you as well."

She sniffled. "At least you don't have to worry about that anymore. I am just an unemployed lawyer."

"What?" His question came with complete shock.

"What, what?" she countered his question.

"You quit your job?"

"You didn't know?"

"Kay said you weren't working. I figured you were taking all your vacation or sick time you had accrued. I had no clue you left."

She nodded. "I did. I couldn't do it anymore. Then I forced Mikayla to fly to Vegas with me. Where I had a breakdown and drank way too much." She rolled her eyes.

"You had some fun though." He tried to show her some positive of it all.

"I did with Mikayla. She can be quite demanding and resourceful."

Shade chuckled because he knew she was exactly right.

"I needed to leave Manchester, even for a day, to realize wherever you are, is where I want to be." She squeezed his hand.

He didn't say anything right away not because he didn't want to but because all his emotions were causing him to forget how to talk.

"And I hope you want the same thing."

Their eyes locked together and remained for several seconds.

"What are you doing tonight?" he asked.

She shrugged. "Nothing. Why?"

"I'd like for you to come to the game and then maybe we can grab some dinner." In truth, his plan was to take her home and lay in bed with her until she fell asleep in his arms. He couldn't care less about the game. Only her.

"Okay. I would enjoy that. It's been a long time since I've been to a game." She gave him a small smile.

Suddenly, his phone began to ring. Pulling it out, he saw Cabel's name on the screen.

"Hey, Cabel."

"Hey, Shade. Where are you?"

"I'm at the park. What's up?" He couldn't figure out why Cabel was curious about his whereabouts.

"Edgar said you needed to talk to me, but I couldn't find you."

Shade sighed. He knew he would have to face this.

"Yeah, I do. I planned on making an appointment."

"You can come up in about thirty minutes. I'll be clear then," he said with the sound of papers shuffling around him.

"All right. I'll be there in thirty minutes." He ended the call, looking over at Jenessa. "I need to run."

"I know. The job of a captain, huh?"

"Something like that." He should have told her why he needed to talk to Cabel but decided not to ruin their time together.

"You really are a great captain," she told him.

He slightly scoffed. "I'm not sure."

"Give yourself some credit, Shade." She touched his shoulder. "You're an outstanding leader."

"Thanks, Jen." Her words meant a lot to him. Just the mere fact she cared meant even more. "Will you come tonight?"

"I already said I would."

"And dinner?" He had to hear her confirmation again.

"Yes, dinner too."

With those words, he stood, and she followed. Together they walked to their vehicles. Like the other night, he desperately ached to kiss her. Instead, he hugged her and kissed her temple.

"I'll see you tonight." He released her and headed toward his truck.

Stepping off the elevator, Shade made his way toward Cabel's office. The secretary wasn't at her desk, but the door was slightly ajar. Shade pushed it open enough to poke his head inside.

"Cabel?"

"Over here, Shade."

Strolling inside, he found Cabel on the couch cradling

his baby girl. His wife, Caryn, sat on the other side of him.

"Sorry, I can come back." He began to walk backward.

"You're okay, Shade. We're getting ready to leave," Caryn told him. "Emilia needed to visit her father before her nap."

Shade looked at the infant. She had Caryn's red hair, but Cabel's face shape and husky build. Baby rolls as Jenessa would call them.

Caryn stood, picking up two bags and tossing them over her shoulders. She reached for the baby, but Cabel moved away.

"Shade, I'm going to make sure they get to the car. I'll be back in a few."

He nodded at Cabel as the little family walked out of the office. The jealousy washed over him. He tried to stop it, but it happened when he saw his teammates with their families. He wished he had a family more than anything. Taking a deep breath, he knew he shouldn't be jealous of someone else's happiness. It was bad karma and he definitely didn't need any more bad luck.

A few moments later, Cabel returned to the office and apologized.

"It's no big deal," Shade said.

"Let's sit and talk." He motioned over to the table.

Shade took the seat across from him.

"Edgar gave me a heads up on what's happening between you and Cat. He said there's more and I'd like to hear it from you." Cabel got straight to the point.

He followed the same suit. Starting from the beginning of their first encounter up until today. He made sure not to leave out any details.

"I already talked to Janan and Nova because I had a feeling about what happened. They spoke to her a little while ago and released her from her position," Cabel explained.

Shade's shoulders sagged with relief. "I have enough going on in my life. I don't need any trouble."

"Cat didn't have the best track record, but they tried to give her a second chance," Cabel said.

He nodded.

"Either way, she's no longer with us."

"Okay. Thank you," Shade said.

"Now, I have another question." He paused and Shade waited to see where the conversation would be going. "How are you and Jenessa?"

"We're talking." He couldn't figure out what else to say. Everything was still in the air.

"Good to hear. If you need anything, let me know." Cabel stood and held out his hand.

Shade did the same and shook his hand. He felt better when he left the office. When he reached his truck, he pulled out his phone.

Jenessa: Thank you for meeting me today. I'm glad we talked. Can't wait to see you tonight.

He didn't know how long he stared at the screen with a real smile.

CHAPTER FOURTEEN
Jenessa

Jenessa couldn't figure out why her nerves were getting the best of her while walking into the family entrance. Not many PHL teams had such an entrance, but the Bears were all about family bonding. They even had a family/friends section.

After giving her name to the security guard, she strolled in, seeing her sister first. She stood with Elexis, her roommate and best friend, who happened to be dating Dag Limon, and Greer was next to her. When Mikayla saw her, she squealed, racing to hug Jenessa tightly.

"Does this mean what I think it means?" She held onto her shoulders.

"We're talking," Jenessa admitted.

Her words caused Mikayla to start jumping up and down and clapping excitedly.

"Who are you?" Elexis jokingly questioned Mikayla.

Instantly she stopped and glared at her. "Don't ruin this moment. I've been waiting a long time for my brother and sister to get back together."

"That doesn't sound right," Greer teased.

"You know what I mean." Mikayla rolled her eyes.

"We're just talking," Jenessa reiterated. "Nothing

more."

"Yet," Greer, Mikayla, and Elexis all said simultaneously.

She didn't reply. She hoped they were right, but she was trying to protect herself a bit. Even though today they seemed to be moving in the right direction.

"Greer!

A tiny voice yelled behind Jenessa. All the women's eyes widened in shock. Jenessa knew exactly what was happening around her.

Greer composed herself and bent down to greet the toddler. "Hi, Klara."

Jenessa stared down at the beautiful three-year-old. The child who had been born a few hours before her son looked up at her. Her heart broke.

"Come on, let's grab our seats." Mikayla pulled on her arm, but she didn't move.

"Hi." The child waved at Jenessa,

Without thinking she bent down to Klara.

"That's my Shade." She reached over and touched the C on her shirt.

"She loves Shade." Nova came up and knelt with everyone.

"He's mine," Klara informed her. "He plays with me."

Hearing this warmed her heart. She'd done everything possible to avoid this child because of the pain it brought her. However, it wasn't this baby's fault and hearing Shade's interactions with her only made Jenessa happier.

"Shade plays with you?" she managed to ask.

"We skate." Klara beamed. Her pale blue eyes shined.

"Since Teo left he's taken her around the rink a couple of times," Nova clarified.

Watching Klara's face it began to blur as the tears came from nowhere. The child's joyous expression changed to concern. She stepped closer to Jenessa, and her tiny hands touched her cheeks.

"Don't cry. Shade will skate with you too. He like

everyone," Klara informed her.

This made Jenessa smile.

"Klara, let's leave Jenessa alone." Nova tried to coax the child away.

"She needs a hug, Mama," Klara said.

Before anyone could stop her, Klara wrapped herself around Jenessa's neck. Feeling the toddler's hug caused the tears to flow faster. Her son would have been the exact same age. Would he have hugged like this? Of course. He'd have Shade's kind and sweet personality. Shade would have taught their son hockey as well. He'd play with him and skate with him, even if he was tired.

"Did I make you sadder?" Klara's tiny lips pouted as she pulled away.

"No. No." Jenessa shook her head. "These are happy tears." She forced a smile hoping the child understood.

"Mama cries during shows," she told them. "She says that is happy tears."

"Exactly," Jenessa agreed.

"Hey, Meatball." Janan came over to the group.

"Jan-Jan," Klara yelled with enthusiasm and ran to Janan.

Janan scooped her up and spun her around. The child's laughter filled the hall. "I'm taking her, Nova." And with that she headed in the opposite direction.

As everyone stood, Nova quickly apologized. "Had I known you were going to be here, I would have made sure she wouldn't have bothered you."

Mikayla handed Jenessa a tissue from her purse. As she dabbed her face, she shook her head.

"No, Nova. You don't have to hide her from me."

"I know it's hard. I don't want you to go through any unnecessary pain since you have enough going on in your life." Nova's sad tone hit Jenessa hard.

All these years, she hadn't been hurting herself or Shade, but everyone in their circle. They all had walked on eggshells around her. Feeling horrible, she hugged Nova.

"You have a beautiful little girl. You don't need to worry about my feelings. Be proud of her." She pulled back.

"We're very happy and proud of her. However, she has Janan's attitude." Nova sighed and the group giggled. "I'm very happy you're here."

"Me too," Jenessa confessed.

"Come on, ladies." Greer cut in. "Let's get some greasy food and watch our men chase a puck."

Laughing, they all began heading toward their seats.

As they sat down with a massive amount of junk food, the game was about to begin. Mikayla and Jenessa shared a large pretzel and nachos with massive cups of pop. She couldn't remember feeling this relaxed. It had been years.

The Bears skated around for their warm-ups. Her eyes landed on him the second he touched the ice. She loved watching him in, what she called, hockey mode. Shade had never been the biggest player on the team, but his determination made up for it. His five-foot-eleven height and one seventy build was muscular, just not bodybuilder size. He made a couple of rounds around the section they were warming up at before stopping and beginning to stretch.

Jenessa's favorite part of the warm-ups. It reminded her of their first time together.

She didn't know much about hockey. All the years she lived in Buffalo; she couldn't believe she'd never gone to a game. Not even a college game. Shade had invited her to a game. When she arrived at the college arena shock filled her seeing all the fans in the stands. She made Mikayla come as well. Not that she didn't trust Shade, but more so she valued her sister's opinion. Mikayla had a great judge of character and could read people better than anyone she knew.

"So, where's Mr. Hot Ass?" Mikayla searched the ice of players

trying to pick him out.

"Right there." Jenessa pointed to the player with the number thirty.

"Nice," she commented.

Then it happened. Shade stopped skating and dropped to the ice. As he began going through the motions, Jenessa's mouth dried, and she gripped Mikayla's arm.

"If you don't fuck him, I will," Mikayla warned.

"Shut up." She slapped her shoulder.

"Girl, look at those moves." She pointed to him on the ice.

"Trust me, I am." Her eyes remained locked on him.

It didn't take long for her to become an instant fan. From the drop of the puck until the final buzzer, she was hooked. She cheered, hollered, clapped until her hands hurt and had the best time she'd ever had. As did Mikayla. When the game ended and they won, Jenessa jumped to her feet celebrating with everyone in the stands.

"Where are we going to meet Mr. Hot Ass?" Mikayla asked as they shuffled out with the crowd.

"Please call him by his name," Jenessa groaned.

"Shade? It sounds like a biker."

"He's not a biker. Stop being so judgmental," she chastised her. "He's a nice guy."

"Sure, he is." Mikayla rolled her eyes. "You don't have a great track record."

"Oh and you do?" she quipped.

"Meh!" She shrugged, making them both laugh out loud.

"Come on, we're meeting him over here." Jenessa moved toward the parking lot when they made it outside.

"Yes, this isn't how every Dateline episode starts," Mikayla grumbled.

"You really need to scale back your true-crime TV time," she told her.

"You sound like Mom."

This made Jenessa groan, and she slapped her shoulder.

"Which car is his?" Mikayla laughed through their interaction.

"Oh!" she exclaimed. "I don't know. I never asked him."

They glanced around the parking lot trying to guess which was his. Jenessa believed it would be a silver Toyota Camry. Mikayla picked the BMW. She knew it wouldn't be that one.

When Shade finally walked out the side door, Jenessa's heart skipped a beat.

"Why is his suit so big?" Mikayla questioned.

"Who cares, Mom?" Jenessa sneered at her comment.

As he walked up to her, his smile grew.

"Great game, Shade." Jenessa hugged him.

He held her for several seconds, then finally let her go.

"This is my sister." She had to force herself to step away from him. Only slightly. "Mikayla, this is Shade.

"What up, bro?" she greeted him.

"Hey." He chuckled.

"We're not hockey fans, but after that game, I could be easily swayed to attend another one," Mikayla blurted out to him.

"I told you. No filter." Jenessa sighed.

"I hope I can keep delivering wins for you, Mikayla." He smirked.

"Great. Now, I'm hungry. Where are we going?" She swiftly changed the topic.

"Maybe we want—" Jenessa started.

"Mikayla, you're more than welcome to come along anytime." Shade jumped in before she could tell her sister to go away.

"See." Mikayla stuck out her tongue at her. "Shade likes me."

This made them all laugh.

"Okay, who's going to drive? Me or you?" she asked him.

"Oh, I don't have a car," he told them.

"Guess Nes is driving then," Mikayla spoke for him.

Jenessa tried to figure out how Shade got around the city. She guessed the bus. It really didn't matter to her. Lacing her fingers with his, they all headed to her car.

"Let's get pizza," Mikayla said as she climbed into the backseat.

"Sounds good. Shade?" Jenessa glanced over at him.

"Sure."

She thought he looked uncomfortable for a second. Playing it off as he might be nervous, she drove the three of them to the pizza parlor. In the car, they discussed hockey, the game, reasons for the penalties, and everything in between.

By the time they arrived at the pizza parlor, they were all laughing and joking around. Jenessa saw how much Shade and Mikayla were getting along like they were best friends. It made her elated to see them cracking jokes at each other.

They walked in, and Shade led them to an open booth. Jenessa slid in first, Shade next her and Mikayla across from them. They ordered drinks and when the waitress left the girls began discussing toppings for the pizza.

"What do you want?" Jenessa asked Shade, who hadn't even picked up his menu.

"Whatever you want," he said with a small smile.

"Pepperoni it is then," Mikayla cheered.

They both noticed Shade wince. He tried to cover it up by taking a sip of his water.

"I'm not feeling it," Jenessa said, and Mikayla agreed.

"Sausage it is then," Mikayla said in the same enthusiastic tone.

From that moment on they laughed, they joked, and Jenessa couldn't remember a time she had so much fun with a boyfriend and her sister. When the bill came, Mikayla grabbed it before Shade. Jenessa was thankful because she had the impression Shade didn't have a lot of money.

When they got back into the car, Jenessa drove Mikayla home.

"Shade, you're my favorite person now, and I'm glad you're going to be my future brother in law."

Jenessa gasped, and Shade chuckled.

"I've always wanted a sister," he told her.

She hugged his neck then gave Jenessa a kiss on the cheek before jumping out of the car.

"She's a nut." Jenessa tried to play off her comment.

"She's pretty cool," he said.

"Um…" She glanced at him. "Is there anywhere else you'd like to go? Or maybe we can go back to your place and watch a movie?" She really hoped he'd take the hint she wanted to go back to his place. The images of him stretching on the ice still played in her head.

"Yeah. Sure. Let's do that."

Unable to tell if he was serious or not, she began driving. Never visiting his apartment, he gave her directions to an apartment building near campus. Shade explained he lived with three other guys.

"It's not the greatest privacy, but they're good guys," he said sadly before opening the door.

There were a few guys in the living room who barely looked up from their video game when he introduced her. Shade took her hand and led her to a long hallway. His door, the second on the left, seemed like a normal door. On the other side, she expected a bachelor's room like the ones she'd been in before, several times before.

She was wrong.

Stepping in, she immediately noticed nothing was hanging on the walls. No movie posters. No athletes. No posters of half-naked women. They were completely bare. Shoved in the corner with mismatched bedding was a mattress on the floor. It appeared to be a full size one to Jenessa but not very thick. Next to it on a milk crate sat a small lamp and a clock radio. Both seemed to be several years old. At the foot of the bed, also on a crate, was a much older model TV.

"If you don't want to stay, I understand," he said, still standing by the closed door.

"Why wouldn't I stay?" She stepped around him. Glancing around she saw the open closet door. Inside there were four shirts, two hoodies, and two pairs of jeans.

"I need to change. Give me a minute." He walked over to a laundry basket setting on the floor of the closet. He picked up a few items and left.

She sat on the bed and scooted back closer to the corner. A moment later, he came back in wearing a pair of sweatpants, which were well worn, and a T-shirt. He carefully hung up his suit before joining her on the bed. They sat quietly. For the first time since their first meeting, there was a bit of awkwardness.

"I don't have much."

Finally, he spoke.

"I'm not taking inventory." She moved her body toward his.

"Is there something you'd like to watch?" he questioned, motioning to the TV.

Even though they only had two official dates, they'd talked every day for almost three weeks. She already knew, if anything was going to happen between them, she'd have to make the first move. He was too sweet and caring to do it himself.

She made the move.

Straddling him, she pressed her lips against his. He gripped her waist and opened his mouth inviting her in. Sliding her tongue over his, they both let out a moan. He grew hard between her legs, and she pressed her hips down onto it. He tugged her shirt up slightly, laying his hands on her hot skin.

As she began rocking her hips, she became wetter. She began pulling at his shirt. They broke apart long enough to get it over his head. He gripped the bottom of hers and stared for a second.

"Are you sure?"

"Yes." She yanked it off for him.

In one swift motion, which made her head spin, Shade put her on her back. Hovering over her, he kissed her jawline before nibbling on her earlobe then moving to her neck. Grazing his teeth over her collarbone, she moaned, arching her body closer to him. Kissing down her chest, he kissed the cups of her bra.

"Hang on," she said, reaching behind her back, unhooking her bra and tossing it to the side.

Shade worked her nipples with gentle bites and sucking. Jenessa was far from being a virgin, but it never felt this good before.

She needed more of him.

"We need to be naked," she panted.

"I agree." Shade lifted his head from her chest.

Together they managed to get naked, the blankets under them.

"I don't want bells and whistles. I want to feel you," she told him.

"Agreed." He reached for his wallet on the milk crate.

She watched him slide on a condom. Enjoying the view of how big he was, she spread her legs for him. As he slid in, she wrapped her legs around his hips.

Jenessa felt the world shake as he pumped in and out of her. None of her other sexual partners ever made her feel like this. Digging her nails into his shoulders, she called his name over and over as his hips rocked harder into her.

"Jen. Jen," he moaned.

Mikayla called her Nes since she could talk. Hearing Shade call her Jen made her feel special.

Her body tensed up then shook as the wave of an orgasm washed over her. Shade pounded into her, stretching out her wave, before grunting out Jen one more time and almost collapsing on her. Easing out of her, he moved onto his side and moved the blankets to cover them.

"I really wanted it to be more special and last longer," Shade managed to say.

"It was perfect." She kissed his lips. A shiver raced down her spine.

"Are you cold?"

"I'm fine," she lied.

"Hang on." Moving the blankets off him, he took off the condom and pulled up his sweats. He rushed out of the room, only to come back a few seconds later. He grabbed a hoodie and another pair of sweatpants out of the closet. He helped her put on everything.

"I could dress myself." She cuddled back under the blankets and curled up to him.

Wrapping his arms around her, she never felt safer.

"You're special to me, Jen." He kissed the top of her head.

"You're special to me, Shade."

"Someone is having dirty thoughts." Mikayla's voice brought her back to the present.

"You think you know me so well." Jenessa tried to play it off.

"Oh, I do, big sister. I also know it's been a *very* long time for you and Shade," she informed her.

"Are you keeping track?" Jenessa quipped.

"All I know is Shade's right arm is bigger than his left. He's certainly tired of playing Whack the Willy."

"Mikayla," she hissed.

"If you just knock the cobwebs off your hoo-ha this might be an earth-shaking night," she continued.

Jenessa dropped her head into her hands, slowing

shaking it back and forth.

"You can be embarrassed all you want, you know I'm right."

Lifting her head, she saw Shade and the Bears moving off the ice. She avoided commenting to Mikayla.

"Stay silent all you want. It only means you know I'm right," Mikayla repeated, leaning in with her sing-songy tone.

Keeping her focus on the ice, the lights began to dim as the introduction video started. She enjoyed the video because it showed all the top plays and players. Shade had been shown numerous times, making her smile with each flash of his face.

The Bears came rushing out of the giant inflatable bear's mouth. Shade was last since he was the captain. Every time she watched him on the ice, his determination was always clear.

When the puck dropped all the guys rushed to gather control of it. Jenessa, as she did every time, watched each movement intently. Especially Shade's moves. He never held an enforcer role, but he did shove players out of the way and into the glass if need be.

The first period brought more excitement than normal. The buzzer had been loud, and the score was nothing/nothing. Jenessa and Greer volunteer to get more drinks.

"It's really great to have you here," Greer said as they stood in line.

"Same." She nodded.

"How are you feeling? I mean, after seeing Klara." She kept her voice low, not wanting anyone else to listen in on their conversation.

"Heartbroken, which will never change. I can't blame her or Nova. Neither of them should run away from me." She hated how they all hid from her. Even though she understood why.

"Are you and Shade going to dinner tonight?"

She nodded. "Yes."

"I heard Mikayla. Has it been a long time?"

She glanced at Greer.

"I'm just being nosy. I'm sorry. It's none of my business," she rushed out the words.

"About a week before I went into labor with Clay," Jenessa confirmed. She thought Greer would pass out right where she stood.

"Three years?"

"Yes."

"Nothing? Nothing at all?" Greer couldn't stop shaking her head.

"Nope. Nothing at all."

They moved with the line.

"Makes me sound horrible, huh?"

Greer furrowed her brow.

"Depriving Shade of sex," she clarified her statement.

"Not just Shade. You too."

Now, Jenessa seemed confused by her words.

"This is going to sound sexist or whatever, but as women, some of us need to be touched to heal. Not only sexually, but comfort as well. I would go out of my mind if Edgar didn't hug or kiss me for three years. Sure, our sex life has slowed over the almost twenty years we've been together but not our signs of affection."

"Oh my God," Jenessa breathed out. Something she never thought about before, but it hit her in the head like a puck.

"What is it? What's wrong?" Greer touched her arms.

"I'm Shade's mom."

"I don't get what you're saying."

"Shade's mother never showed him affection or love. I'm the only person who ever truly had. Then what do I do?" she questioned.

"You quit showing him affection and pushed him away," Greer answered.

"And treated him like shit." Jenessa wanted to kick her

own ass right now. "All these years I treated him like his mother had."

"*And* now you can change it," she reminded her.

"You're right. I can." Jenessa became renewed with a newfound determination.

After they got the drinks and went back to their seats, Jenessa began to think about Shade's pain. She imagined his childhood and all he went through. Only for her to drag him through the same emotions.

To use Mikayla's words, she was a royal bitch.

Jenessa managed to go through the motions of the game. Cheer when everyone else did. Boo when everyone else did. Give the signature Bears' growl when everyone else did. All the while mentally chastising herself for all she did to Shade.

The Bears won by one point and the crowd went wild. They now sat in the top five of the PHL. Jenessa moved with the rest of the family out of their assigned door, back down toward the hallway off their locker room.

They all stood around chatting, waiting on the guys, when Elexis made a comment.

"Is Janan wearing bigger clothes for a reason?"

Everyone who heard the question turned to study the co-owner of the Bears.

"She seemed to be fine," Greer said.

Jenessa continued to inspect her as she moved around talking to the family members. She couldn't put her finger on it, something was off with Janan. When she made it over to their group, she was eyeing them.

"Are you all talking about me?"

"Yes," Mikayla answered as the rest said, "No."

"We were wondering what's up with the outfit?" Mikayla pointed at the attire.

"I came over here to talk to Jenessa." She ignored Mikayla.

"What for?" Jenessa couldn't think of what they would have to discuss together.

"I heard from your gossipy sister, you're unemployed." She thumbed over at Mikayla.

Jenessa rolled her eyes. "Who didn't she tell?"

"We need an attorney. You up for it?" Janan blurted out.

"Janan," Nova called her name as she strolled over to the group. "When will you learn how to be civil?"

"What?" she gasped.

Nova faced Jenessa. "I apologize. Let me explain this situation in a more professional manner. Janan and I have several charities we've started over the past year. Our regular attorney who helped Uncle Oliver is retiring. This has made us begin searching for someone to replace him. Recently, we learned you had left your position and currently are not with another firm. We'd kindly like to extend an invitation for you to look into our current open position and let us know what you think." Then Nova glared at Janan. "That's how you do it."

"I did the same thing. Only with fewer syllables," Janan said sarcastically.

"Wow, thank you for thinking of me." Jenessa was seemingly shocked by the offer.

"I can email you the job description," Nova added.

"Please do. I'll look it over and let you know as soon as possible."

Just then the players began making their way out of the locker room. A few moments later Shade, Edgar, Jarvis, and Dag came out together, strolling over to their respective female. As the others greeted each other with hugs and kisses, Shade gave Jenessa a smile.

"Great game."

"Thanks."

"Let's go eat," Jarvis announced and the crowd began

heading toward the door.

Jenessa gripped Shade's wrist halting his movements. "Could we go home?"

Shade studied her face for a second. "Are you sure?"

"Please," she begged.

"Absolutely."

She noticed he tried to hide his smile.

"I didn't drive. I Uber'd over." She did hoping he would take her home tonight.

"I'm ready when you are."

Without thinking or worrying about what he'd think, she took his hand into hers. He gave her hand a gentle squeeze and led the way to the truck.

Their conversation had been light. They discussed what to eat and Jenessa used Grub Hub to have Mexican waiting for them by the time they arrived. The rest of the talk had been about hockey. She could hear his excitement about the Bears being back on top again.

Once they were in the house, Shade took off his jacket and tie and rolled up his sleeves. Not long after, the doorbell rang as Jenessa poured two glasses of water for them. Shade answered the door and brought the food over to the breakfast bar. He set everything out for them as she took a seat.

"Thanks for coming to the game," he said.

"Thank you for the invitation." She handed him a fork.

As they ate, Jenessa told him about the offer from Nova and Janan.

"What does it all entail?" he asked taking another mouthful of food.

"Truthfully, I have no idea. Then again, it's not like I have offers banging down the door." She tried to make it a joke, only to make her sound more pathetic.

"Don't take the job if you don't want to. You'll find the one you want."

Shade was always the one to be supportive of her and her career. He never forced her into a job or taking on more cases.

"It could be interesting to work for Nova and Janan. Especially working with charities. Did you know they started them?"

He nodded. "We sign a lot of merchandise for them to be auctioned off." He closed his almost empty container and wiped his mouth with a napkin.

Jenessa stared at him for a few seconds before he looked over at her.

"Do you want me to leave?" he asked.

Certainly, he would think that because of the way she'd been treating him.

"No. Why don't we go into the other room?"

"Okay."

They went into the living room and sat on the couch. Jenessa tried to think of where to begin. So many emotions ran through her. Not to mention, all the revelations.

"What's wrong, Jen?" He finally broke the silence.

"Something came to me tonight and I need to discuss it with you. Most of all, I need to apologize to you," she started. Turning her body, she tucked her legs behind her.

"What do you mean?" He watched her carefully.

"Greer and I were talking tonight, and I realized just how big of a bitch I've been to you. I know you'll never say it to me but let me get all of this out."

Shade nodded in silence, waiting for her to continue.

"I can't even begin to say how sorry I am for the pain I have caused us in the past three years. I can't explain how broken I was and still am. I just wanted our baby." She closed her eyes, trying to keep her composure.

"Jen, I, more than anyone, understand your pain. I'm just as broken. The pain is still heavy in my heart. I want nothing more than to have our son here. I'd give up everything for him to be toddling around us."

Opening her eyes she knew by his expression, he meant it.

"Shade, I'm your mother," She blurted out.

"What?" He scrunched his face in confusion.

Waving her hands, she tried to invisibly erase the already said statement.

"I'm mean. I'm causing you pain *like* your mother. I have pushed you so far out of my life and closed myself off. I don't know if I can fix it. Or if you even want to be in my life?"

"Jen, you're not my mother. Nor will you ever be like her. What we're going through is a horrific tragedy. We can get through it together."

His words touched her. However, she couldn't allow him to continue to be in this misery.

"Shade as much as I want our future to grow together, I don't know how to fix all of this." Now she waved her hands around them.

Instead of replying he stood up and paced around the room. Jenessa never remembered him pacing. This was completely out of character. She remained quiet until he stopped.

"Jen, I don't know how to fix this either. However, I know we're not good apart. First, you're not my mother. Yes, you caused me a lot of heartache, but you had a reason. She just up and left me one day. I was only eight years old. Second, we will have a future together as long as we both want it and fight for it. It won't happen overnight, but it'll happen. I know it." He had a calm tone as he spoke.

"You left for a reason though. The pain became too much," she said.

"I left because I thought it would make you happy again," he clarified.

She jumped up from the couch and over to him. "You need to be happy. You deserve it."

Shaking his head, he deeply sighed. "Why are you acting like this?"

"Like what?"

"You're pushing me away. *Again*. Only this time, you're doing it to my face." His calm tone wavered with the anger growing on his face.

"I can't make you happy because—"

"Enough!" he roared, causing her to take several steps back.

In the ten years they've been together, he never ever raised his voice. He may have been frustrated with her but never yelled at her.

"Fucking enough, Jenessa. I have loved you since the second I laid eyes on you, I knew I would marry you after our first date. You are my heart, my air, my soul. Yes, you have broken my heart. You have stomped on it. You have pushed me out of your life. But I'll be damned if I let you do it anymore without hearing me out."

She remained frozen as he continued in his loud tone.

"I would do anything for you. You want me to leave? I will. You want me to stay? I will because I want to be here with you. Our future will be happy. I know it. You just have to believe it too. Stop pushing me away, Jenessa. Give us a chance."

Still standing in place, she stared at him. He had always expressed himself in the complete opposite manner. He told her to give them a chance. Every part of her was scared but wouldn't pass on this moment.

Taking three strides, she reached up, grabbed the back of his neck and pulled him down to her lips. It took Shade a couple of seconds to relax. He gripped her hips and pulled her closer to him. Opening her mouth, she welcomed his tongue into her mouth. They moaned in unison. It had been three years since they last touched each other in such an intimate way.

She didn't know how she got to the couch on her back, but she could not care less. Shade's body covered hers, and she felt safe. Running her fingers through his hair only made their kissing intensify. Finally, they both were forced to come up for air. They stared at each other for several seconds, breathing heavily.

"Never doubt how much I love you, or how much I want our marriage to work." His voice cracked as tears filled his eyes.

"I don't want to hurt you again." Fear began to creep up in her.

"As long as you talk to me and let me help you, you'll never hurt me."

Jenessa couldn't stop the sobs that seemed to come from nowhere. Shade maneuvered to put them on their sides and let her cry into his chest. Soon the crying slowed and eventually stopped, allowing her to fall asleep in his arms.

CHAPTER FIFTEEN
Shade

Blinking several times, it took Shade a second to figure out what was real and what had been a dream. He remembered carrying Jenessa up the stairs after she fell asleep in his arms on the couch.

"You're awake."

Turning his head, Jenessa was laying on her side facing him.

"What time do you have to be at practice?" she asked.

"It's optional."

"You're not one to play hooky." She smirked.

"Typically, no. I'm willing to make an exception today." He mirrored her expression.

"I have errands to run today. Want to come along?"

He noticed how hopeful she sounded. He could miss one optional practice. "How about we go for a run first?"

"Perfect." She rolled off the bed and went to the bathroom.

Shade sat up as reality set in. There were no clothes of his to change into since he'd been living at Jarvis's condo. Should he move back in? Did she want him to? He decided not to rush it and let it all work out on its own.

She stuck her head out of the bathroom. "Give me five

minutes, then we'll run to the condo."

"Okay." He wondered if she'd recently become a mind reader.

He went downstairs and found his phone. He texted Hamilton letting him know he wouldn't be at practice. When he went to the kitchen, he poured himself a glass of orange juice. Last night replayed in his head. A roller coaster of emotions put him through a lot. He never yelled. Especially at Jenessa. Albeit, something snapped, and he lost it. He hated how she compared herself to his mother. Nothing could be further from the truth. Yes, they'd been through a lot, but it was nothing like what he experienced with his mother. Jenessa would never be cruel like her. They'd lost their son. His mother was a junkie who couldn't handle any responsibility but to get high.

"Are you okay?"

Her beautiful voice broke into his thoughts. Lifting his head, his stunning wife stood in front of him.

"Yes, I'm good."

"I'm ready when you are," she announced.

He moved toward her, giving her a small kiss. Picking up his tie and coat, they walked out to his truck. When they arrived at the condo, Jenessa said she'd wait in the truck while he went up and changed. Thankfully, no one was around, so he didn't have to avoid any questions.

Once he changed and made it back to the truck, he drove them to the park. Their conversation hadn't been anything in-depth. She never mentioned the divorce papers or him moving back in. Therefore, he didn't say anything.

Jenessa jumped out of the truck first after he parked it. They stretched together before starting a light jog to warm up. Then they picked up speed. He always thought she was a great runner. He loved when they would go on runs together. Even though they never said much during the time, they would still have fun.

"I'll race you to the tree," she said. "Loser has to buy

lunch."

Before he could say deal, she yelled, "Go." He let her have a couple of strides on him, but his legs were much longer. Just as she was about to reach the tree, he grabbed her waist, causing her to squeal. He placed her behind him and passed the tree. Holding his arms up in victory, he bounced from foot to foot.

"You cheated," she called him out.

"I call it adapting to completing the task. Counselor," he joked.

She pushed on his chest as she passed him moving toward the truck.

"I'm thinking surf and turf for lunch," he continued to tease.

"Whatever." She playfully rolled her eyes, hopping into the truck.

"What's next?" he questioned.

"I need to run to the store and the mall. If you want to come, I'd enjoy it." She smiled.

"I need to shower and change." He commented.

"Just drop me off at home and come back when you're ready.

He pretended he wasn't hurt by her words. He preferred going home with her, but he had no clothes or soap to take a shower because he didn't live there anymore.

"Great."

After dropping Jenessa off, he rushed back to the condo and hurried to get ready. He wanted to get back to her as quickly as possible. He was almost afraid she'd change her mind.

When he made it back to the house, he didn't just walk in. He rang the bell. It took several seconds for Jenessa to answer, but when he saw her fresh face, all anxiety about her changing the plans went away.

Her smile said it all.

"Give me ten more minutes." She rushed back up the

stairs.

Shade took a seat at the breakfast bar and checked his texts and emails. When she came back down she was casually dressed in skinny jeans and a dark hoodie. Her hair was piled on top of her head in a bird's nest.

"Want to grab food first?" she suggested.

"Yes." He stood.

"I'll drive." She picked up her purse and keys as they made their way to her car.

On the way to the diner, Jenessa asked about the upcoming holiday events. He knew she'd been around enough to realize it would be becoming hectic soon. When they arrived at the diner, he was surprised to see it practically empty. Then again, it was a weekend morning. When they sat down, they both knew what they wanted and ordered it once the waitress came to their table. After she left, Jenessa began discussing the weather.

"I figured it would be snowing by now," she commented.

"Yeah, I thought so as well," he added.

"Maybe we take a trip to Alaska or Canada. Doesn't skiing sound fun?"

Shade stared at her for a second. A bit taken aback about her talking of vacationing together, he simply nodded. He took her ideas as a positive sign for their future together.

"Would you like to go to the winter party with me?" He didn't give himself much time to think it over.

Jenessa smiled. "I'd love to."

He tried not to jump up and down. This would be their first event together since before Clay's death. She had tried to attend after he'd beg her, but it never happened.

Their conversation moved to hockey. Over the years, Jenessa had grown to enjoy the game and was able to easily converse with him. When the food came, they ate in silence, enjoying the meal. However, he noticed Jenessa kept looking over his shoulder with a confused expression.

"What's wrong?"

She leaned toward him and lowered her tone. "I'm used to people recognizing you and being star-struck."

This made him roll his eyes. A habit he picked up from Jenessa and Mikayla.

"But this girl two tables back is throwing daggers at us."

When he looked over his shoulder, his stomach dropped at the face staring back at him.

"Oh, fuck," he groaned, putting an elbow on the table and rubbing his forehead.

"Who is she?" Jenessa inquired.

"A fucking pain in my ass," he told her.

"Well, get ready because she's coming over," she warned.

Just then Cat appeared at their table, her hand on her hip, glaring at him.

"Thanks for getting me fired," she snapped.

"I told you to leave me alone." He sat back, crossing his arms.

Instead of answering him, she turned her attention to Jenessa. "You the wife?" She sneered.

"Yes," Jenessa answered in a calm tone.

"Well, he's a lousy lay."

Shade's world began to spin out of control. He couldn't believe what she said. "I never—"

Jenessa's hand came up to stop him from talking. "*If* you slept with *my* husband, what does his tattoo say?"

"What?" Cat turned up her nose.

"It's a simple question," Jenessa countered, still not raising her voice.

"That's a trick question. He doesn't have any," Cat said proudly.

Jenessa smirked. "Yes, he does. He has my name and our son's name over his heart. And if you *did* sleep with him, you wouldn't be calling him lousy."

Shade had always been proud to wear their names but

rarely ever showed a bare chest.

"So *you're* lying. Now get away from our table. If you contact *my* husband again, I will get a protective order for him. Then you'll have to stay away or go to jail."

Cat's face paled. They stared at each other for a few more seconds before Cat turned and rushed out of the diner.

"Care to explain?" Jenessa picked up her fork.

He'd planned on telling her all about Cat. However, his focus had been on them and nothing else. Shade started from the beginning and their first encounter. He left nothing out. He told Jenessa about how uncomfortable she made him feel, going to Kian, having the conversation with Edgar there and finally Cabel telling him she'd been let go.

"Wow," Jenessa said when he finished. "Do you want to do something legally?"

He shook his head. "As much as I should, I just want her to go away. My focus is on us now. I was going to tell you about her."

"Shade, if there's one thing I know more than anything, it's the fact you tell me everything and truthfully."

He relaxed after she finished. It meant a lot to him she still trusted him.

"We have to get to the mall and get some shopping done." She smiled, changing the subject.

Shade paid the bill, even though Jenessa tried, and together, hand in hand, they walked to her vehicle and drove to the mall.

Shade never considered himself a shopper. In fact, he barely shopped at all. The reason he came along today had been just for her. He carried the bags, commented on everything she tried on and gave his opinion on the

Christmas gifts she purchased for Mikayla. After the mall, they hit the grocery store. Again, he pushed the cart, bagged it all up and carried it to the car.

When they made it back to the house, Shade felt exhausted. Mainly because of his emotions. He had so much he wanted to ask *and* say but didn't dare ruin the moment they were in. He put the groceries away and she put away everything else. This made it feel like old times. Something he craved again.

Putting away the last item, he went into the den and stretched out. He just needed to lay down for a second. After a few minutes, Jenessa strolled in, leaning over the sectional she grinned at him.

"You can play hockey all day and night, but a few hours shopping, and you're wiped."

Checking his watch, he stated, "We shopped for almost six hours."

"Ppphhh." She motored her lips and waved her hand. "Amateur."

This made them both laugh.

"Come lay with me for a minute." He hadn't meant for the words to come out. Merely think them. However, they were out there now.

"Okay." She came around the sectional.

Shade maneuvered onto his side as she mirrored him. Resting one hand on her cheek, she placed the other on his chest. Shade had tucked one arm behind his head and left the other at his side. Normally, he would put it on her hip, but again he didn't want to rush anything or ruin this day.

"Do you think about having more kids?"

Her question came out of nowhere.

"Yes," he answered truthfully.

"With me?"

Shade glanced down at her in shock and confusion. "Who else would I have them with?"

She shrugged. "Probably someone else."

"There's no one else. Nor will there be," he firmly told

her.

Slowly she moved her eyes up to his. "What if we divorced?"

A hot knife of pain just stabbed directly into his heart by her words. The 'D' word hung between them and sat heavily in the air throughout the room.

"Then I would leave, but I'd never be with anyone else. You're my everything, Jen. You're the other half of my soul. You're my world. Just like I said last night." He kept his eyes on hers, not even blinking. She had to hear his words again and feel them.

Instead of her saying anything to him, she dropped her head, snuggling closer to him. Even though he wasn't going to move his arm resting at his side, he changed his mind. Wrapping it around her waist, he pulled her to his chest and kissed the top of her head.

Closing his eyes, he tried to figure out a way for this moment to never end. He'd hold her forever if she asked him. He'd leave if she asked him to. No matter how much it broke him. Whatever she needed—or wanted—to be happy again, he'd do it for her.

A shiver ran down Shade's back, causing him to open his eyes. He focused trying to recall where he was and what was happening. It all came back to him. Spending the day with Jenessa and falling asleep in each other's arms.

However, she was no longer on the sectional with him.

Slowly, he stretched out his tight muscles and stood up. Searching the first floor of the house, she wasn't there. Making his way up the stairs, he stopped at the top of the steps. There, at the end of the hall, sat Jenessa. In front of their baby boy's closed bedroom door. There were several tissues in her lap, and he heard the soft sniffles. He gently walked over to her and sat next to her. He let her talk first.

"I think about him every single day," she began in a tiny voice. "I wonder what he would look like. Even though I know he would look like you." She softly giggled.

"He had your nose and ears," Shade said, thinking of his son.

"He did, didn't he?" She glanced over at him.

"He'd probably have Mikayla's attitude," he joked, breaking the tension.

Jenessa rolled her eyes. "You're probably right." And they both laughed.

"Most of all he would be loved and happy," Shade added.

She nodded.

They sat there in silence, both staring at the door. Both thinking about their son.

"Would I have been a good mom?" Jenessa asked after a couple of minutes.

"You would have and will be the best mother any child could ask for." Shade took her hand in his.

"It's my fault, Shade." Tears fell fast from her eyes.

Immediately, he pulled her into his lap, wrapping his arms around her. He wished he knew a way to take away the pain and give her joy back.

"Jen, it's not your fault." He tried to reassure her. Peppering her hair and forehead with kisses.

"I was his mom." She cried into his chest.

"And I'm his dad. My job is to take care of both of you." The noticeable crack in his voice came with tears burning his eyes.

Lifting her head, he felt the warm tear slowly slide down his cheek. She scrambled out of his grasp, only to straddle his hips. She hugged his neck.

"I'm scared, Shade," she said through her sobs. "I've caused you pain. More pain than anyone should ever endure. All because of me."

He held her tightly, and his tears flowed faster.

"I'm sorry. I just hurt so badly because our baby's

gone." She buried her face in the crook of his neck.

"Jen, look at me."

She pulled back.

"We're always going to miss him. We will always have pain. But we have more love for each other. This will get us through all of it. We just have to remember we're a team. Forever."

CHAPTER SIXTEEN
Jenessa

Seeing Shade's tears broke Jenessa's heart more than she ever thought. Through the hurt she caused him, he still loved her. For the past three years, he never wavered from her. She couldn't blame him for leaving. Hell, she could barely stand herself during those worst days.

"I love you, Jen. I've never stopped. I never will." More tears came from them both.

"I love you, Shade. I'm sorry. I didn't know how to handle my pain. I just lashed out and pushed everyone away," she confessed, sadly.

"I'm right here. You can never push me out of your life. You're my everything." He cupped her face.

"We have a broken marriage."

He shook his head. "No. It has a crack. A fixable crack. One I want to fix. I want to come home to my wife."

His emotions hit her hard. She felt his love and desire. Not just to come home or fix their broken marriage but for her. She felt his lust and love for her.

Leaning in, she gently pressed her lips against his. She felt safe with him. As if he could wash away all the problems in the world.

When they broke from the kiss, she laid her forehead

against his. "I love you."

"I love you, Jen."

She knew exactly what to do next. Pushing herself off the hallway floor, she reached for his hand. Easily he took her invitation and stood up. She led them into the bedroom. *Their* bedroom.

Shutting the door behind him, she grew slightly nervous. Even though she had thought about sex these past years, it frightened her at the same time. Becoming pregnant again was not on her to-do list, but right now the thought didn't even cross her mind at all. She just wanted to show him how much she loved him.

Gently, she pushed him to sit on the bed. She saw the dried tears on his face. Holding up one finger, silently telling him to wait. She went to the bathroom to get a warm washcloth. She wiped her face clean before grabbing a fresh one for Shade. Coming back out, she walked over to him and carefully cleaned his. This reminded her of the many times he bathed her the couple weeks following Clay's death.

When his face was clean, she began to softly kiss his cheeks first and then his lips. A fire burst through her as their kiss intensified. Shade's hands ran up and down her body. Opening their mouths wider, each moaned as their tongues battled.

Breaking away for air, she took a small step away from him and lifted her hoodie over her head. Shade removed his shirt next. Her eyes landed on his left pec. There, still in the blackest of inks, against his naturally tan skin was her and Clay's name. She traced both with the pad of her finger.

"You're beautiful."

Shade's voice broke into her trance.

"I need you." The lust she felt for him clearly came across in her voice.

He rose to his feet. Standing in front of her, he didn't move. She knew the game he played. He always waited for her to make the first move. His stomach clenched as her nails ran down his abs. He wasn't cut like some of the other players. However, one could clearly see the outline of his abs.

With her eyes locked on his, she managed to undo his belt, unbutton his jeans, and pull the zipper down. Heat rose through her as her heart beat faster.

"You're not going to last long, are you?" she questioned. His entire body was tense. The expression he held told her everything without him saying one word.

Slowly, he shook his head. She saw him swallow hard. His chest rose and settled with his soft erratic breathing. Shade had always been a sweet lover. His concerns for her always came first, never worrying about himself. However, there were times he let himself go. He manhandled her, roughly pounding into her, but never hurting her or crossing a line she hadn't allowed him to cross. She enjoyed every experience with him.

"Just let go."

The phrase was one they both used when they spiced up their bedroom activities. Because there had been times she been not so gentle with him as well.

"Jen, I can't...can't tonight." His husky tone sent shivers through her. "It's been too long, and my hormones might get the best of me." He struggled to hold himself together. His grip bit into her upper arms. Again, not hurting her.

"Please, Shade. It's been so long since I felt you deep inside me." Her fingers toyed with the band of his boxer briefs.

She knew she was egging him on. After all these years she could push the right buttons to set him off in the best way.

"You win." He gruffly growled out the two words before picking her up and tossing her onto the bed.

She gasped, and Shade already covered her body with his. Spreading her legs and raising her hips, she felt him pressing his hard cock down on her.

"I need more," she begged, tugging at his jeans.

He rose up and took her pants off, leaving her completely naked from the waist down. Only leaving her bra on. The wildness in his eyes turned her on even more. He pulled his jeans and boxer briefs down to his mid-thighs, freeing himself from the confines of his pants. As her hand grabbed him firmly, she began to stroke him.

"You have to stop, or I'm going to blow on your stomach," he told her with a strained expression.

"That's not where I want it done at." She spread her legs again, removing her hand.

Shade growled. Actually growled. Now, he gripped himself and bent down to her. Lining himself up with her opening, she watched Shade hesitate for a second. She touched his cheek.

"Please, Shade."

Those two words were all he needed to set everything in motion. She expected him to slam into her. Almost preparing for it. However, Shade pushed about halfway in—slowly. He'd given her body time to adjust. Jenessa moaned loudly as she felt him. She'd deprived her body of his touch for such a long time, she forgot how great it had been to feel him again.

"More, Shade. More." Her brain barely remembered how to form words.

He complied. Pushing all the way in, they both gasped. Her body stretched, but she didn't feel any pain. Only pleasure.

"Jen."

She knew what *that* meant.

"Let go, Shade. Please."

And he did.

He pounded into her hard enough to knock out all the air in her lungs. Arching her body to feel every inch of him, she panted. This was the only way she could get any air. Her body relaxed, but then immediately tensed. She felt the wave of an orgasm coming. Like a tidal wave. She hadn't felt this in a long time. Calling his name over and over, pushed her over the edge. Her body shook with pleasure. Even through her ecstasy, she heard him call out her name, feeling his release deep inside her. Shade collapsed onto her, but for only a second.

"Sorry," he managed to breathe out and moved onto his arms.

"Stay." She pushed him back down onto her, not wanting to be without his closeness.

He kissed her lips ever so softly, saying how much he loved her over and over. With his weight on top of her and the warmth of his touch, Jenessa's body fell into a peaceful sleep.

Jenessa felt someone playing with her hair. She'd been having the best sleep. Slowly opening her eyes, Shade stared down at her.

"Good morning," he said.

With confusion, she glanced around. The sun illuminated the room. "What time is it?"

"Seven in the morning."

She realized she was under the blankets, still in only her bra. "I've been asleep for almost ten hours?" She would never stay in bed this long unless she was sick.

"Yes. Don't worry I've been asleep almost as long," he admitted. "And I hate to leave you right now."

"Why?" she questioned with a panicked tone.

"The plane leaves in a couple of hours. I have to go."

Realization came rushing back. Shade had to play hockey. "How long do we have?"

Checking his watch, he said, "Forty-five minutes. Hour tops."

A sly smirk appeared on her face as she rose up and

kissed Shade. Feeling down his body, she figured he was naked. It was the way he always slept. When her hand found what it was searching for, she realized he was almost hard, and she began to stroke him.

"That gives me plenty of time." She flirted before maneuvering to straddle his hips.

"I love you on top," Shade moaned as she glided down his shaft.

Like last night he stretched her but didn't hurt her. Slowly she began moving up and down finding the perfect rhythm. Placing her hands on his chest, she used her grip to keep her balance. Shade grabbed her ass, guiding her pace.

"Shade." She tossed her head back, completely taking every inch of him.

Rocking her hips faster, she stared deep into his eyes. His brown eyes turned her on even more. His eyes were full of...love. Only for her. Always for her. Together they found the release they both missed giving each other. She fell onto his chest and immediately he wrapped his arms around her.

"I love you, Shade."

"I love you, Jen."

As the high of their quickie wore off, her legs tightened. Easing off Shade, he wouldn't let her go far. She curled up on his side. They laid still holding each other, not saying anything. Only enjoying each other's touch.

"I don't want to ruin our moment, but there's a question weighing on me."

Jenessa propped herself up to see Shade's face. "What is it?"

He didn't look at her right away. It took several seconds for him to face her.

"Do you want me to move back in?"

Jenessa had to blink a couple of times to make sure she heard him correctly. Sitting up further she tried to process his question. In her mind, they worked all of this out last night. Apparently, they hadn't.

"I think the bigger question is, do *you* want to come home?" she countered wanting to hear what he had to say.

Shade rose and rested his back against the headboard. "I've told you several times, I want you. This includes coming back here to live. However, I don't want to push you either."

She appreciated him for putting her first. Then again, he always did.

"Shade, I can't promise you it's going to be a perfect ride. I still hurt every day. I don't have a job. I'm an emotional mess. But you belong here. We belong together."

Shade leaned over and kissed her. "All I ask is you talk to me, lean on me, and I'll do everything in my powers to take your pain away."

Meeting his lips with hers, their love flowed between them. She missed him, which caused her even more heartbreak. They needed to rebuild themselves and their relationship.

"But I do have to go," he told her, sadly.

"You could quit, and we can just stay home forever. You know, live off the land."

Shade laughed. "You mean Grub Hub?"

Trying to act offended, only caused her to begin laughing harder. A real laugh. One thing she hadn't done in so long. In between their laughter, they continued to kiss.

Eventually, they left the bed. She slid into a robe as he dressed in the same clothes as yesterday. They were just about to walk to the kitchen when they heard the ding of the microwave.

Together, they said, "Mikayla."

Sure enough when they reached the kitchen, Mikayla sat at the breakfast bar, watching a knitting video on her iPad.

Jenessa tapped her shoulder. "You don't live here," she

told her when she pulled out one of her ear pods.

"And?" she questioned as if there would be an extensive explanation to come.

Rolling her eyes, she gave up and went over to the Keurig to make her coffee.

"If you must know. Elexis and Dag wanted a morning alone," she explained.

"Why didn't you go to Jarvis's?" Shade asked the same question she thought.

"He and Joy haven't been spending quality sibling time together lately." She shrugged. "She needed some brotherly time."

"What's in the microwave?" Jenessa opened the door.

"Oh." Mikayla rushed over to it. "My mac and cheese."

"It's seven-thirty in the morning," she told her.

"So? I'm hungry." Mikayla shrugged again and took the bowl. "Don't be jealous because I can cook better than you."

"It's a microwaved mac and cheese. I can handle that." Jenessa barked at her. She saw the look of 'no way' from Mikayla as she flashed it to Shade, who only smirked. "You both are assholes."

This made all three laugh and Jenessa turned to fix her coffee. Shade and Mikayla talked about whatever knitting video she was watching.

"Well, ladies, as much as I hate to say it, I have to leave." Shade pushed off the breakfast bar.

She knew he would be coming home tomorrow. And *really* coming home to her.

"I'll walk you out," Jenessa said.

As they began to walk toward the door, Mikayla loudly cleared her throat.

"I'd like to clarify *I* was the glue that put you two back together. Which means I should get a hug, or a new car, or maybe a diamond bracelet, or a gift card. Something showing some gratitude." She faked a pout.

Instantly, Shade went over to her and gave her a hug

and a loud kiss on her forehead. "Do you feel better now?"

"Meh," she said before smiling.

"Love you too, sis," Shade said as he made his way back over to Jenessa.

She always loved their relationship.

When they reached his truck, he gave her a kiss. "I don't have much to move back into the house. I'll get it all gathered when I get back into town tomorrow." He grinned.

"Okay. I'll be here." She kissed him again and watched him climb into his truck.

After he drove away, she went back into the house. Mikayla remained seated in her same spot.

"I'm guessing you've been having a whole lotta sex." She winked, taking a bite of her food.

"Actually, just twice," she corrected. "And he's moving back in."

"I'm glad," Mikayla said with deep sincerity.

Taking a deep breath, she confessed what weighed heaviest on her. "We didn't use anything."

Quickly, Mikayla eyed her with concern. "Are you okay?"

"Worried. Scared. Ready to burst into tears." She ticked off her emotions one by one.

"Don't go there," Mikayla commanded. "You're happy again. It's been three years since I've seen you this happy. Don't let fear ruin it for you. Or for him."

Jenessa nodded, but *that* fear crept right up her spine and rested in her brain. Her thoughts ran wild through every possible scenario. Mostly the worst ones.

"Do you want Shade?" she asked.

"Yes." She didn't hesitate with her answer.

"Then you need to enjoy this time. Reconnecting with your husband is the number one priority. If you get pregnant, we're all going to celebrate. But don't ruin this for you or him."

Staring at her coffee, she tried to focus on the good. Shade. Shade was what brought the best out of her. He did for everyone.

"It sucks I won't see him until tomorrow." She sighed.

"I remember a time you used to surprise him on road games," Mikayla reminded her.

This made her giggle. Any chance she could take she would hop on a plane and go to a road game with him. She loved to support him. They'd joked their pregame sexcapades would help him play better.

Mikayla clicked off the knitting video and opened flights from Boston. "You could get on a plane and be there in about four hours. Practice would just be about over by then."

"Book it," Jenessa said as she raced to the bedroom to get ready to see her husband.

Yet again, Mikayla pulled off another traveling miracle. She drove Jenessa to the airport in just enough time for her to be one of the last people to board the plane.

Once she landed, she debated about renting a vehicle or Uber-ing to the hotel. When she saw the line to rent a vehicle, she decided she was going to Uber. However, luck would have it, numerous cabs were unoccupied when she stepped out of the airport.

Mikayla had already booked a room for her. All she had to do was check-in. The room was nothing spectacular, but it had a big bed.

Grabbing her phone, she had to find out where Shade was right now. Shade had been texting her all the while she was at the airport and in the plane. She didn't want to hint to the fact she was coming.

Jenessa: What are you doing? How did practice go?

He answered faster than she figured.

Shade: Practice was good. We're on the bus, heading to the hotel

She smiled at the screen.

Jenessa: Are you going to lunch with the guys?

She figured more than likely he would have made plans.

Shade: Nah. Going to relax a bit. What are you doing?

She knew it would be the perfect time to answer his question.

Jenessa: Oh, not much. I'm in room 504 at the Marriott hoping you'll come hang out with me.

It took a minute for him to answer.

Shade: What? You're here?

Jenessa: Yep. I thought you might need a pregame workout *wink*

Shade: I'll be there in ten minutes. Unless I jump off this moving bus and run. Then it'll be five minutes.

Jenessa laughed at his text. Setting her phone to the side and reaching for the room service menu, she ordered two large chef salads. She knew he would be hungry and needed to keep his strength up.

About fifteen minutes later, the food came to the room. She set everything on the small table and then ran to get some ice. As she came down the hall after retrieving the ice, Shade was standing outside her door.

"Excuse me, are you waiting for someone?" she teasingly asked.

Shade, dressed in workout gear, turned to her. A sly smirk on his face.

"I'm waiting for my stunning wife who came to surprise me."

She felt the blood rush to her cheeks. "Well, she sounds wonderful."

"You have no idea how perfect she is."

His words shot right through her in the best way. Even

after all they've been through and the way she treated him, he still loved her.

CHAPTER SEVENTEEN
Shade

Shade wanted to pinch himself to make sure this wasn't a dream. Then again, if it were one, he didn't want to wake up. He couldn't remember being this happy. After all the pain and sadness from the past few years, he felt loved again. By the one person he wanted to be loved by the most.

His wife.

When she opened the hotel room door, he had to restrain himself from throwing her on the bed and burying himself inside her.

"I ordered food for us." She set the ice bucket down on the tiny table with two massive trays. "Do you want to eat first?"

He couldn't explain what happened next, even if he tried. His hormones controlled him. It was the best way to say it. Shade gripped her wrist and guided her to the bed. He never ever made the first move. Today would be an exception.

Gripping the bottom of her hoodie, he pulled it over her head. She said nothing. Only studied his every move. Unhooking her bra, she tossed it to the side. Their eyes remained locked for several seconds. Slowly, he knelt onto his knees and pulled her jeans and underwear off as well. She stepped out of them, leaving her absolutely naked.

He kissed in between her breasts, moving his hands up her soft skin, he cupped her breasts. His lips captured her hard nipple, gently pulling it with his teeth. Jenessa moaned, running her hands through his hair.

"Shade."

Hearing his name off her lips made his cock even harder. It begged to be released behind his sweats. Kissing down her flat stomach, he pushed on her hips, making her sit on the side of the bed.

"Lay back." His rough tone came from all the sexual arousal in his body. He couldn't hold it back anymore. Even though they've had sex twice in the past twenty-four hours, he hadn't shown her how much he missed her.

She did as he said.

He placed one kiss on one hip and then another. Her legs opened for him and a moan escaped her. She knew exactly what he wanted. He licked her slit, and her body tensed up.

"Shade."

Spreading her legs wider, Shade sucked on her most sensitive bud. Jenessa withered under him, calling his name and moaning. Those noises were the most beautiful sounds to his ears.

Sliding one and then a second finger into her, her wetness drenched his hand. He began to find the rhythm he wanted. The one where she arched her back, pulled his hair and panted out his name.

She fulfilled everyone of them.

His mouth and fingers were soaked. He loved he could still get her off. She remained on her back trying to catch her breath. He rested back on his haunches, wiping his mouth and watching her.

"It's my turn." She rose up and motioned him with her forefinger to come closer.

Shade stood up and Jenessa smirked.

"Take off your shirt," she demanded.

He did.

Jenessa tugged down his sweats, freeing his erection, and he felt a bit of relief. Tiny bit. He ached for her touch. Now, she got down onto her knees in front of him. He couldn't be sure his legs would keep him upright for what was about to happen next.

As she grasped him, she kept the hold firm but without hurting him. When she began to stroke him, he let out a deep growl. Shade tried to think of anything to keep his mind off of coming too soon. He wanted to make this last as long as possible.

She stopped stroking only long enough to lick his entire shaft. Then she placed him in her mouth, almost swallowing him. He had to hold onto her hair to remain standing. Tossing his head back her mouth picked up the pace, sliding up and down his length.

"Jen," he breathed out.

Staring at her, he watched her beautiful mouth on him. Like before, his hormones took over, and he began to move deeper into her mouth. Her jaw went slack, and he took over. Holding her head, he pushed until he knew she couldn't take anymore. The faster he went the closer he was about to come.

"Jen?" he growled out her name, but she knew there was more to it.

Looking up at him, she opened her mouth as wide as she could. He knew she was silently giving him permission.

When they first started having sex, Jenessa had come up with the idea of living out a fantasy at least once a month. She probably thought Shade was a prude because his sexual fantasies weren't groundbreaking. The big one Jenessa enjoyed the most was about to happen...

Right now.

With a grunt, he felt himself coming deep into her mouth.

They didn't move for several seconds before he eased

back and sat on the bed. Jenessa rose and went off to the bathroom to rinse her mouth. He pulled the blankets back and waited for her.

When she strolled over to the bed, she crawled in right next to him, curling under the blankets.

"That was fun." She smiled.

"I'm so glad you're here." He kissed her forehead. "I always loved it when you surprised me."

"I loved it too. Hopefully, I can do it more since I'm still unemployed," she joked.

He knew she hated not having a job. He didn't worry about her not finding one. He wanted her to do something she loved.

"Have you heard from Janan or Nova about the job?"

"Not yet. They may have changed their mind." She shrugged.

"I'm certain you'll hear from them soon." He tried to reassure her.

Jenessa didn't reply, only snuggled closer. He wrapped his arms around her. This was home to him. Holding her meant the world to him.

"Your belly's rumbling," she teased running her fingers on his stomach.

"It'll stop." He did not care about his super mild hungry pains.

"Come on, Shade. Let's eat." She moved from his hold and began getting dressed.

He held back his disappointment, leaving the bed and sliding into his sweats. Sitting at the table, they began to talk about nothing and everything. Shade's well-hidden elation kept him focused on her every word. She told him her flight left in the morning, and he wished there was a way she could hop on the team plane.

After he finished the massive salad, he yawned.

"Time for a nap," Jenessa commented.

"I'm good," He lied.

"Come on." She stood, grabbing his hand and leading

him back to the bed.

Once his head hit the pillow, he remembered nothing else.

Shade definitely didn't want to wake up nor leave the comfort of Jenessa's body pressed against his. However, he had to.

When he walked into his hotel room which he shared with Jarvis, he was greeted by wooting and catcalling from him.

"Someone smells like sex and happiness." He winked.

Shade only smirked. Giving Jarvis an inclination about what went on would only be fuel to his fire. Instead, he moved about the room to get ready.

"Hey, in all seriousness, congrats, man," Jarvis offered.

He looked over at his friend. "Thank you, Jar."

"I guess this means you won't be using your hand as much." Then the real Jarvis returned.

Shade rolled his eyes, grabbed his suit and began to get ready for their game tonight. Once dressed, he packed up his items since they would be leaving right after the game. He tried to think of a way to get Jenessa on the plane, but nothing came to mind. Janan was with the team today while Nova stayed back in New Hampshire. Maybe he could ask her. All she could say was no.

A knock came on the door which meant the time had come for them to leave. They began to make their way out of the room and into the hallway with the rest of the team toward the bus. In the lobby, he caught a gaggle of ladies wearing Bears' merchandise near a large fireplace. He saw Padge, who recently became engaged to Gage. Erin. Who dated Bas. Baylor, who was with Alden and Greer. Then his eyes landed on his wife. Her back was to him, but he knew it was her. Her hair sat on top of her head. Instead of it being messy, it was a smooth ponytail. Her brown hoodie had *Wooten* on the back, and it made him smile. Then the ladies turned to see the guys strolling through the lobby. Jenessa's eyes found his and all he felt was love.

They were going to be okay.

Shade couldn't believe this game. Glancing up at the jumbotron he felt his mouth twitching into a smile. Five to one with Bears leading, and he held two of those points. Everyone on the team seemed to be on fire.

"This is crazy," Edgar said next to him "You want that hat?"

Shade nodded. "Jenessa's here." His short response should be enough for Edgar to understand.

"Let's go," he yelled as they jumped the boards.

When his skates touched the ice, a second wind hit him, and his body took over. He swore he could feel Jenessa's eyes on him. He wanted to get this point for her and the win. Even he never had two hat tricks in a season, it would truly be a long shot.

But dreams could come true.

It felt like a slow-mo video on YouTube as the play played out in front of him. Vance passed the puck to Jarvis, who passed it to Edgar, who turned and chucked it over to Shade. He knew to be ready. Pulling his stick back, his eyes didn't leave the puck coming toward him. As his momentum began to move forward his blade hit the puck at the perfect point. He watched it sail through the air over the left shoulder of the goalie and into the net.

Shade threw his arms in the air as his teammates rushed him. He hugged them, slapped each other on the helmet and was completely overjoyed. He couldn't believe it really happened. He had another hat trick.

For Jenessa.

The rest of the game was a complete blur. Thankfully, there hadn't been much time left. In the locker room, everyone celebrated. Patting Shade on the back, they all congratulated their captain.

After getting out of his pads, doing several interviews, showering, and getting into some fresh clothes, Shade and the rest of the team were ready to get on the bus.

The excitement began to wear off when he hit the seat on the airplane. He hated that Jenessa remained there for the night, and he would be back in New Hampshire. However, the positive side of all of this, by the time she landed, he would be moved into the house.

Suddenly, an idea popped into his head. Quickly, he pulled out his phone and texted the one person who could help him with it.

Shade: Kay, I have a favor to ask.

Jenessa: I'm boarding the plane. Love you!
Shade: Can't wait to see you. I love you too!

Shade put his last piece of clothing into his duffle bag.

"You think your plan is going to work?" Mikayla asked. She sat in the center of the bed.

"Yes, as long as you do your part."

She tilted her head side-to-side as if she'd been thinking extremely hard.

"Yeah, I think it will too," she finally said, easing his mind.

"Let's get to the house," he told her, zipping up the bag and tossing it over his shoulder.

When they reached the house, he put away his stuff. With each shirt and each pant he hung in the closet, his smile couldn't grow any larger.

He was home.

"I found it," Mikayla yelled from downstairs.

"Great," he hollered back and jogged down to her.

She held the manila envelope in her hand. When she handed it to him, he wanted to rip it up right then. However, it wouldn't work in his plan.

"I'm going to get to the airport. I'll see you soon." Mikayla waved as she headed out.

Shade glanced around the house and felt at home. He only hoped his plan would work.

Sitting at the table, Shade didn't feel nervous at all. He only worried about what Jenessa would say. Would she think this was dumb?

Originally, he would be drinking coffee, but since he quit drinking caffeine, he had a decaf hot tea with lemon in front of him.

When he saw them walk into The Latte Bean, Jenessa looked stunning in the sweater, skinny jeans, and knee-high saddle boots. He never understood how she grew more beautiful with every day that passed. Mikayla led her to the booth next to his table.

"What's going on?" Jenessa asked. "Why are these tables listed as reserved?"

"Stop asking so many questions," Mikayla groaned in frustration. "Just think where you were ten years ago and figure it out." She literally shoved her into the booth then turned to Shade.

"Good luck." She waved and left them.

"Shade, what the hell is going on?" She leaned on to him, but he ignored her.

It was killing him not to speak to her.

The waitress rushed over with a French vanilla cappuccino and a cherry turnover.

"I didn't order anything," she told her.

"No, but this is what you had ten years ago. Or so I'm

told." The waitress winked and rushed away.

"Wait," she breathed out in shock.

Shade tried his best not to look over at her as she just figured out he was recreating their first meeting. He couldn't help it. Glancing over to her brought him back to *that* moment they met.

"Stood up?"

Jenessa smiled at him. "Would you like to join me?"

When she asked the same question all those years ago, he had the same reaction. He wanted to jump over the table to get to her. Instead, he calmly stood and moved over to her booth.

"Shade, what's going on? For real," she inquired with a serious tone.

"You still hate surprises, huh?" He grinned.

"You know I do." She pushed everything to the side.

"You win." He nodded and knew it was time to lay it all out on the table. Literally.

"Since the day we met, I have been in love with you. After our first date, I wanted to marry you. Even with everything that's happened, my heart and soul still belongs to you." Hidden under his jacket he pulled out two large envelopes and set them on the table.

"What are these?" She stared at them.

"Divorce papers," he said.

Her eyes flicked up at him. "Why do you have them?"

"The worse thing I ever did was leave you that night. I should have stayed and told you exactly how I felt. But I thought it would be best for you, even though it broke me."

He saw the tears in her eyes.

"I told the attorney to draw these up because—again—I thought it would be best for you. My goal is to make you happy. However, I don't want to divorce you. This is our marriage and I want to be with you. No matter what the future holds. We'll be together."

Jenessa studied his face. "Shade, I've loved you more

than anyone in my life. Minus Mikayla because she is in her own category. I knew right away we were meant to be together. So much has happened in our ten years together, we really should write a book."

Shade chuckled, agreeing with her.

"A divorce isn't what either of us need or want."

Hearing those words was like seeing a rainbow after the worst rainstorm. He watched as she picked up one of the envelopes and ripped it in half. Then she did the same with the other one.

"Let's go home." She slid out of the booth and held out her hand to him.

As he took it, he knew they would have a happily ever after.

CHAPTER EIGHTEEN
Jenessa

After leaving The Latte Bean, they rushed home to get out of their clothes and into bed. Jenessa couldn't remember the last time they'd spent all day in bed.

When Shade fell asleep, she watched him. His handsome face, strong jaw, and eyelashes, she'd pay money for, made her heart flutter. His words still spun in her head. His romantic side always shined more than hers. She never would have thought of trying to re-create their first meeting.

Slipping out of the bed without disturbing him, she put on her robe to head to the kitchen. As she stepped out of the bedroom, she should have turned to the left, but her body went right. Noticing Clay's door was open, she slowly made her way to it. The last time she actually stepped foot in the nursery had been the day before she gave birth to her baby boy.

Leaning against the doorframe, she studied every inch of the room. She remembered how she bitched at Shade to make sure everything was absolutely perfect, and he made it happen.

"Jen?"

She looked over and saw Shade in his boxer briefs

standing near her.

"Why are you crying?" He padded over to her, wrapping his arms around her and kissing the crook of her neck.

"I'm thinking." She sniffled and went back to the doorway. "We need to do something about all of this, don't we?"

"No." Shade stood behind her, placing his hands on her shoulders. "We can keep this here however long you want."

Moving to face him, she said what worried her the most. "We've been having a lot of sex."

"I know. Do you want to stop?" he said with deep concern.

"Not particularly," she said, honestly.

"I'll get some condoms," he assured her without hesitation.

"I'm scared. I'm worried. I'm full of anxiety even thinking about getting pregnant," she confessed.

"Jen, I'm all those emotions as well."

She placed her head on his chest. His strong beating heart brought comfort to her. "You don't have to wear condoms."

Saying the words out loud didn't mean the emotions and fears just disappeared. But somewhere, deep down, she did want another baby with Shade. She wanted to be a mom.

Moving away from his warmth, she took a step into the room. Slowly making her way to the crib, she saw the small urn in it. The memories of her labor and his birth made the tears fall faster. The pain of knowing he died could never be put into words.

"I've been thinking," she started, wiping her tears.

Shade was right next to her and rubbed his hand up and down her back.

"At the park, you can buy those benches and put a plaque on them. What if we got one by the play place and spread his ashes around?" She hated thinking of his ashes locked up in the tiny urn.

"That's a beautiful idea." He kissed her forehead.

"Let's donate everything." She looked over at the closet full of clothes, blankets, and everything in between.

"Whatever you want, Jen." He kept his lips resting on her skin.

"We're fixing our broken marriage," she breathed, feeling some relief off her shoulders.

"One crack at a time."

When his lips touched hers, she felt the world melt away.

BECAUSE I KNOW MY READERS
WANT TO KNOW

EPILOGUE
Four Months Later
Jenessa

"I shouldn't be nervous." Jenessa still laid in bed as Shade moved about the room getting ready for practice.

"Janan and Nova believe in you. *I* believe in you. Hell, even Mikayla believes in you." He stopped moving and came over to her. "You can do this." He kissed her lips. "Call me if you need me."

She watched him leave and waited for the front door to close. Quickly, she texted Mikayla.

Jenessa: He's gone. Hurry.

This afternoon, the Bears' legal team would be sitting down and going over the contracts for the players. Now, on top of being a part of the Bears' legal team, she had been given the task of being the attorney to work on Janan and Nova's charity. However, there was something bigger on my mind.

"I'm here," Mikayla yelled as she came in.

"Up here," she hollered.

"Why are you still in bed?" she asked when she came into the bedroom.

"Because I have to pee so badly. If I stand, I'll need to go right then," she explained as her bladder begged for relief.

"I've got 'em." Mikayla jerked a bag out of her large purse and dumped several boxes onto the bed.

"How many pregnancy tests did you buy?" Jenessa gasped.

"Ten."

"Why?"

"We want to be sure. Oh." She yanked out a red solo cup from her purse. "Use this."

"What is happening here?" She stared at the cup now in her hand.

"Pee in the cup. Put all the tests in there and boom, we have a definite answer." Mikayla laid out her idea as if she'd been planning it all her life and was finally able to unveil it to the world.

"I asked you to help me to keep me from losing my mind. This," she waved her hand over everything, "isn't helping me."

"Okay." Mikayla held up her hands. "I'm here for you. Whatever you want."

"Thank you." She finally stood up and her bladder protested in moving at all. For a second, she stared at the cup and all the boxes. Sighing, she said, "Fuck it," and gathered up everything and went to the bathroom.

After she finished and came out, Mikayla set the timer on her phone. They sat on the side of the bed in silence for several seconds.

"Don't go there," Mikayla spoke first. "Don't let your head spin out of control."

"I can't help it." She sobbed.

Mikayla held her tightly, and it brought comfort to her. Unable to stop the tears, she let them fall.

"Jen, I'm back." Shade's voice boomed through the house. "I forgot my wallet."

She heard him coming toward the bedroom. When he stepped in, he immediately stopped.

"What's going on?" He rushed over to her. "Are you

okay?"

Then the ding of the timer answered his question.

"Stay with her," Mikayla told him as she got up from her spot.

"Jen, talk to me," he begged.

She stared at him for several seconds. "I love you."

"I love you too. But you were fine ten minutes ago. Tell me what's going on. Talk to me."

"I might be pregnant," she said the words through her tears.

Shade's face paled.

"And I'm scared," she continued.

"Me too, but it's going to be okay. We're in it together." He kissed her lips, but she clearly saw how he felt. He was scared as well.

Mikayla walked back into the bedroom, and they both looked at her with anticipation.

"You're pregnant."

This would be the time where they would be rejoicing like they did with Clay. However, this time, Jenessa broke down in tears.

Shade

Shade called Cabel and took a healthy scratch day. Jenessa told him she *had* to go to work. But one call to Janan, and it allowed her to come in later. She still had to be there before the afternoon meetings. Then Shade called Jenessa's OB/GYN. Thankfully, and by a miracle, the doctor could see them almost immediately.

"Mikayla, are you coming?"

Shade heard the plea in his wife's voice. He knew she needed them both to stay calm.

"You're stuck with me." Mikayla smiled trying to be strong for her. But Shade saw her wavering.

The three of them piled into Jenessa's car while Shade drove them all to the doctor's office. The ride was silent, and Jenessa never released her hand from his. Time seemed to move fast for Shade. Once they arrived at the office, they were called back within minutes.

Dr. Franklin walked in. She was a thin black woman who looked to be forty, but Shade remembered her saying she was in her fifties.

"Hi, everyone," she greeted them and went over to Jenessa. "It's going to be okay," she told her in a soothing tone.

"I don't know." She shook her head and squeezed Shade's hand tighter.

He didn't care if she broke every bone in his hand if it made her feel better.

"Let's run some tests and do an ultrasound. I'm going to list you as high risk. Even though your last pregnancy had no issues except during labor. We're going to pull out every precaution this time," she assured them.

"I want to discuss a scheduled c-section," Jenessa blurted out.

"I was going to suggest the same," Dr. Franklin said.

"What's that?" Shade asked.

"We'll pick a date to do a c-section instead of Jenessa going through traditional labor and delivery," she explained.

Shade liked the plan a lot.

"We'll discuss it more the closer the due date approaches. First, let's get some blood work and an ultrasound." With another smile to them she headed out of the exam room.

A nurse came in and took Jenessa to get the blood test done. When she left, Shade collapsed in a chair. Mikayla came over to him and held his hand.

"You can be strong for her again. This is going to be a good thing," she told him.

"I know. I'm worried about her."

"As am I. For you both. But you're going to get through this. As is she."

Shade nodded. Somehow Mikayla always knew what to say at the right time.

A few minutes later, a nurse came in to get Shade and Mikayla and led them to the ultrasound room where Jenessa was waiting on the table for them. He went to her and grasped her hand.

As they prepped her for the ultrasound, he leaned down and kissed her softly.

"I love you."

"I love you," Jenessa said.

"Okay, here we go," the tech nurse said.

Shade stared at the screen. It only took a few seconds before the grainy image appeared. All three gasped as the profile of a tiny baby appeared.

"Is the baby okay?" Jenessa choked out the words.

"Everything looks great," she told them in a bubbly tone. "You look to be about ten weeks."

"Really?" Jenessa questioned. "I thought I might be six weeks at best."

"Not according to these measurements," she told them. "I'll be sure to print out plenty of pictures. Dr. Franklin will be in shortly."

Once Jenessa was situated back in her clothing and sitting upright, Dr. Franklin came back in and went over a few things. She wrote her a prescription for some prenatal vitamins. And said she'd see her in four weeks.

When they arrived back at the house, Shade studied Jenessa's face.

"Mikayla, give us a minute," he said. After she got out of the car, he said what was on his mind. "Please don't shut me out."

Jenessa turned to him. "I'm not. I promise. Right now, I'm all over the place in my head trying not to think of what *could* or *couldn't* happen during all of this."

"Trust me. I'm feeling the same." He sighed.

"We can get through this."

He wasn't sure if she asked a question or if it was an

encouraging statement for them both. Either way, he kissed the back of her hand.

"We will. Together."

Thirty weeks later

Jenessa

Everyone around the table laughed at Jarvis's answer.

"I know I'm right," he hollered above the roaring laughter.

Shade, Jenessa, Mikayla, Jarvis, Edgar, and Greer sat around the table. The game 'I Should Know That' was on the table. The teams were girls vs guys and the girls were winning by far.

"You three are cheating," Jarvis mumbled, pouting and crossing his arms.

"No reason to be a sour butt." Edgar slapped his shoulder.

Jenessa rubbed her swollen belly as she watched the interaction. Her pregnancy had been smooth. She had numerous breakdowns throughout, and Shade had been there for her every single time. However, starting last night she had some of the worst back pain and was very uncomfortable. She tried to ignore it, but it seemed to grow worse. Ignoring the pain had been somewhat easy since tomorrow was her scheduled c-section. This was the reason why everyone came over tonight to celebrate with them.

The doorbell rang and everyone began to clean up the cards. Their food had arrived.

"I'm starving," Jenessa announced as Shade headed to grab the subs they had ordered.

"Didn't you eat twenty minutes ago?" Mikayla called her out.

"Shut up." Jenessa slowly rose to her feet. She had gained thirty pounds during the pregnancy, and her large belly kept throwing off her balance. Not to mention, her swollen ankles.

"Where are you going?" Greer questioned.

"To refill our drinks," she informed her.

"I'll help," Greer and Mikayla said in unison, both jumping out of their seats.

Jenessa shook her head but didn't argue. She knew they were doing it out of love. In the kitchen, she leaned against the counter. She took a deep breath in as a pain shot through her.

"What's wrong, Nes?" Mikayla rushed to her side.

"The small of my back is still killing me," she moaned. "Poor Shade rubbed it for over an hour last night and again this morning."

"How long has it been like this?" Greer asked.

"I don't know. Forever it seems like but probably more like twelve or fourteen hours. It's nothing though." She waved it off. "Hey, Greer, what's going on with you and Edgar?" She noticed there was a bit of tension between them when they arrived.

"Nothing." She clearly gave them a fake smile.

"Really?" she pushed.

"It's been hard since our daughter left for college, and our son is a high school senior. We're beginning to feel the empty nest," she explained with a sad tone.

"It'll just give you two more time together." Jenessa tried to show the positive side.

"Right." Again Greer smiled but clearly forced it. "You know, I really wish you and Shade knew what the sex of the baby is. I could have planned an outstanding gender reveal party."

Jenessa knew she changed the topic on purpose, and she wouldn't pressure her about it anymore. "We decided to be surprised this time."

"And they're not telling *anyone* the names they've chosen." Mikayla glared at her.

"We want everyone to be surprised," she reiterated.

"I'm the baby's aunt. I should be a part of everything," Mikayla exclaimed.

Jenessa laughed at her outburst, which reminded her of Jarvis.

Then it happened.

She felt a *pop*.

And her underwear and jeans were soaked.

"Nes? Nes? What is it?" Mikayla touched her arm.

"Oh my God, her water broke," Greer exclaimed.

Panic flooded her and her knees almost gave way. "Shade. I need Shade," she whispered her command, afraid to move.

"Shade!" Mikayla yelled.

"What?" He ran into the room.

"Her water broke. I'm going to call the doctor." Mikayla took charge as he rushed to her side.

Jenessa's entire body began to shake as Clay's labor and delivery flashed through her mind.

Shade must have realized what she was thinking. "Jen, it's going to be okay."

She felt herself nodding, but no words were coming out.

"Okay, the nurse said to go to General Hospital asap. They're going to alert the ER we're coming," Mikayla announced. "I have your bag, purse, phone, and keys. Let's go."

"We'll clean up and lock up," Jarvis told them as they began making their way to Jenessa's car.

Mikayla hopped into the driver's seat as Jenessa and Shade got into the back. Jenessa wouldn't let go of his hand. As hard as she'd been trying to keep the panic attack at bay, it was starting to be a losing battle. Shade kept saying it'll be okay over and over.

As if they were in a stock car race, Mikayla made it to the hospital in record time. Pulling up to the emergency room door, Mikayla jumped out and ran into the hospital. Just as Jenessa stepped out of the car, a nurse appeared with a wheelchair.

The pain seemed to grow around her body more and more. It made her squeeze Shade's hand only tighter. He never complained once. She was wheeled to the labor/delivery wing and whisked into a room. With the help of Shade and the nurse, her clothes were removed, and she was put into a hospital gown.

Once the machines were all hooked up, the attack hit. She couldn't stop the tears, the fear, and the unknown.

"I'm scared," she finally spoke through the sobs.

"I'm scared too." Shade put his forehead on hers. "We're going to do this together."

"You won't leave." She sniffled.

"I'm never leaving you. Ever." He kissed her.

"Where's Mikayla?" She glanced at the door as if she'd appear out of thin air.

"She's parking the car. She'll be here shortly." His explanation appeased her for a moment.

Pain shot through her, and she twisted trying to make it go away. She kept breathing, hoping it would help, but it didn't seem to at all.

The nurse came back in and needed to start an IV. Jenessa really hated IVs, but right now her pain levels were off the chart. She could not care less as long as they gave her something before they took her for the c-section.

Once it was in, Mikayla made it to her room. Jenessa felt a bit better having her and Shade with her during all of this.

"You can stop having all the fun without me." Mikayla winked at her.

"I'm…I'm…" Jenessa stammered over her words.

"Stop. Don't think about anything but delivering this baby," she consoled Jenessa.

Jenessa nodded.

Several minutes later, Dr. Franklin finally came into the room, dressed in scrubs. "I hear your water broke."

"Yes, about forty minutes ago," Shade said.

"How's the baby? When are you going to do the c-section?" She rushed out her questions to the doctor.

"Let's check a few things," Dr. Franklin said. She checked the readouts on the machines. She gave the nurse a couple of instructions then put gloves on her hands. "I'm going to see how dilated you are."

Jenessa assumed the position as the doctor rooted around her most private of areas. She just breathed through another contraction.

"Jenessa, how long have you been having contractions?" the doctor asked while discarding the gloves.

"I haven't felt anything until I got here," she told her.

"No pelvic pain? No back pain?" Dr. Franklin continued her questioning.

"She has been having back pain since the middle of the night," Shade interjected.

"She's been having it all day," Mikayla added.

The doctor's face dropped, and she faced Jenessa. "We can't do a c-section."

Her heart fell to the floor. "Why?"

"You're already dilated nine centimeters, Jenessa. I can feel the top of the head. You're going to have to have a natural delivery."

Panic hit her like a tsunami. She couldn't breathe as she began to drown in her own fears. Gripping Shade's shirt, she started begging him.

"Please, don't make me. Please, Shade. I can't do this again. I can't handle it."

She gasped for air but couldn't find any in the room. All her brain was telling was the baby would die. Like Clay. She knew her heart and soul couldn't handle losing another baby.

"Jenessa." Dr. Franklin's normal bubbly professional tone had left. Now, a firm, almost drill sergeant-like tone made an appearance.

Opening her eyes, she looked at her doctor.

"I promise you. I will do everything in my power to have a successful delivery. I'm going to have a crash cart ready and more nurses on standby. But *you* have to do your part. Look." She pointed at the monitors. "The baby is *not* in distress, but you are. This might put the baby in danger. Do you understand? I need you to calm down."

She nodded, trying to breathe normally.

"I'm going to get everyone ready. Your baby should be here soon. If you feel like you need to push before I get back hit the red button." With those parting words, she left.

Mikayla and Shade kept trying to soothe her, but the ringing in her ears kept her from actually hearing them.

"I'm scared. I...I... can't do this." She forced the words out in between sobs.

Shade sat on the side of the bed cupping her face. Looking deep into her eyes, he said, "You're the strongest person I know. Whatever happens, we're going to do this together. You can do this. *We* can do this."

She nodded, and he kissed her lips.

"Here." Mikayla patted a cool washcloth on her forehead and then wiped away her tears. "You're doing great, Nes. Just keep taking deep breaths."

Nodding, Jenessa did as she said. After taking several cleansing breaths, her heart calmed slightly.

"Stay positive," Mikayla said, still trying to keep her cooled down with the washcloth.

Jenessa kept breathing as the pain grew. Then, as if being placed in a tub of freezing cold water, every alarm went off in her body.

"I have to push. I need to push." She felt all the blood draining from her. This was happening, but she didn't know if she could do it.

Shade pushed the alarm and almost instantly Dr. Franklin and five nurses appeared in front of her. Everyone was hustling around the room. Nurses were putting these flimsy yellow gowns on Shade and Mikayla.

A cap was placed on Jenessa's head.

"Jenessa, bear down," Dr. Franklin ordered.

Shade and Mikayla helped her scoot down the bed and then they practically folded her in half. At least, she felt as if they had. Pushing with every muscle she could find, her body began to react.

"Okay, relax. Take a breath," the doctor said.

Jenessa collapsed back on the bed. Her ears were ringing again. There were numerous people staring at her, and Dr. Franklin barked out some more orders.

"One more time, Jenessa."

Tears burned her cheeks as Shade and Mikayla pulled her tired body back into position. Both of them cheering her on, but she only had one focus.

Her baby.

She pushed and pushed until she felt the baby slide out. Looking down she saw the horror of her premonition. The baby was completely purple with the cord around the neck.

Then her world went black.

Shade

The nurse standing closest to Shade shuffled him away from Jenessa. Mikayla rushed to his side as his knees gave way at everything happening around him. She managed to get him into a chair.

"Shade, calm down." Mikayla held him.

He couldn't stop the tears or the sobbing coming from deep within him. Jenessa passed out as soon as the baby came out. He saw what she did. The cord around the tiny baby and then he lost it.

"Shade, stop crying and fucking listen. Don't fucking make me slap you." She shook his shoulders trying to get him to focus.

"What, Kay?" he snapped loudly at her.

"Shut up and listen." She didn't seem fazed by his outburst.

As he was about to argue, he heard it.

A baby's cry.

Shade jumped to his feet, but Mikayla grabbed his arm. "Let the nurses work.

"Is the baby okay?" he asked them.

"She's perfect. Just needed a little suction," one of the nurses informed him.

"She?" Mikayla looked up at him. "It's a girl?"

"It's a girl," another nurse announced and the cries grew louder.

No sweeter sound touched his ears before than his daughter's cry.

"How's Jenessa?" he asked Dr. Franklin.

She walked over to him. "She's passed out but stable. The smelling salt brought her around for a few seconds, but she fell out again."

"And the baby?" Shade pressed wanting her to reconfirm what the nurses had said.

"The cord wasn't wrapped around tightly. Jenessa grows a long cord," she half-joked

"She's an overachiever," Mikayla cracked.

"If she gets pregnant again, what can we do?" Shade asked.

"Nothing. It's biology. However, next time we'll do a c-section at thirty-eight weeks." She smiled. "Your baby is healthy and loud. Which is a great sign. Jenessa should be coming around in a few minutes. I gave her something to perk her up. Congratulations."

Shade kept his eyes between his daughter and wife. He desperately wanted to hold them both.

"Mr. Wooten?" the nurse called out.

"Yes?"

"Do you want to hold your daughter?"

He and Mikayla rushed over to where the beautiful baby laid. His heart stopped as his eyes landed on his daughter.

"You can pick her up," the nurse urged. "Here." She

lifted his daughter and gently placed her into his arms.

He couldn't express how he felt at that moment. His baby looked tiny in his arms but love filled every inch of him.

"She looks like Jenessa," Mikayla commented peering at her niece.

"We'll take her now." The nurse reached for the baby and Shade immediately took a step back and Mikayla stepped in between them.

"Why?" they both asked.

The nurse softly laughed. "We need to clean her up. We'll be right back with her."

"You can watch from the nursery," the other nurse added.

"I'll go. You stay with Nes," Mikayla volunteered.

"We'll be back very soon," the nurse reassured him as he handed over his baby girl.

Under his watchful, protective eyes, he studied them as they all walked out of the room. He moved over to Jenessa's bed and wiped his face free of the tears that kept coming. He got the wet washcloth Mikayla used earlier and began wiping Jenessa's face. Even though her makeup ran all over her face, she was still stunning. He cleaned her up then grabbed a clean washcloth and continued to pat her face.

Several minutes later, Jenessa began to stir. When she opened her eyes, they locked onto his.

"Hi," she said softly with a small smile.

"Hey, Jen." He grinned back.

Then, as if a light switch had been turned on in her head, she gasped and began scanning the room. "Where's our baby?" She grabbed her stomach. "Where's our baby?

"Listen—"

"No." She wailed gripping his shirt. "Please don't tell me." She sobbed harder into his chest.

"Jen." He pushed her off him, trying to get her to focus on his words. "Jenessa, look at me." Now, he understood what Mikayla went through with him.

"No. No. No." She shook her head not opening her eyes.

"She's alive, Jen. Our daughter is fine." He repeated himself three times before she figured out what he'd been saying.

"What?"

"Our daughter is alive. She's perfect," he said again.

"Wh…what?" She began looking around the room. "Where is she? Where's our baby?"

"The nurses are cleaning her up. Kay's with her. She'll be back soon."

"Is she okay? Because I saw it, Shade. I saw it wrapped around her throat." She motioned to her own neck.

"I know. I saw it too. It wasn't tight. She could breathe," he explained.

Now, her tears came with a smile.

"She looks like you, and she's loud like Mikayla."

Jenessa laughed. "But she's real, right? I'm not dreaming."

Cupping her face, he kissed her lips. "She's real. This is a dream come true. One we've waited for for many years." He kissed her again. "Lay back and rest. She'll be here soon."

Nodding, she did as he said. But he knew she wouldn't be able to rest until she saw their daughter.

"How are you feeling?" Shade asked her.

"Tired. Sore. But happy." She squeezed his hand.

"I'm happy too." He placed his lips on her knuckles.

"How are you?"

"Well, I had a breakdown on that chair and Mikayla almost slapped me to get out of it."

"Why?"

"Because I thought the same thing you did." He cleared the lump in his throat at the fresh memory. "I thought we lost her."

Jenessa moved his hand up to her face, laying her

forehead on it. "I think we've had enough pain in our lives to last five lifetimes." She reached up and softly wiped a stray tear off his face.

Just then the door opened, and he heard Jenessa gasp as Mikayla walked in. Behind her was the nurse pushing a hospital bassinet with their daughter inside.

"I kept my eye on her the whole time. We aren't going through some switched at birth bullshit," Mikayla informed the room. "And the nurse here wouldn't let me carry her." She shot a glare over her shoulder.

"We have policies," the nurse said. "Enjoy. We'll be in to check on you again shortly."

Mikayla picked up the baby making cooing sounds as she handed her to Jenessa. "Baby No Name Girl, here's your mommy."

Shade watched Jenessa's face as the baby was placed in her arms. Everything they went through was for this moment. True, undeniable love filled her eyes and face as she saw their daughter.

"Oh my, she's perfect," Jenessa breathed. "Shade, isn't she perfect?"

"Yes, she is."

With Shade's voice, their daughter's eyes opened.

"Look at her." Jenessa stared at her.

"She looks a lot like you," Mikayla commented.

"Actually, she reminds me of you," Jenessa said, glancing over to her sister.

"One thing is for sure, she doesn't have Shade's nose." Mikayla smirked.

"Back off, Kay. I've had a couple broken noses in my life," he told her with a friendly glare.

"I think there's a bigger issue here than Shade's odd shaped nose," Mikayla said in a serious tone. "What is this beautiful baby's name?"

Jenessa looked over to Shade with a bright smile. "Do you want to tell her?"

Shade grinned. "Mikayla Marie, please meet Kayla

Marie."

Mikayla's face turned white. "Wait, what?"

"We decided to name her after you." Jenessa touched her sister's hand. We love you, and you're the best third wheel ever."

Tears filled Mikayla's eyes.

When Shade and Jenessa talked about names they immediately knew they wanted to use Mikayla's name in some form or fashion. She'd been the *black sheep* of the family and was always cast to the side by her parents. Shade knew Jenessa protected her as much as possible. When Shade came into the picture, he loved Mikayla instantly. He never thought of her as a third wheel. And like Jenessa, he always looked out for her.

"Thank you," Mikayla managed to say as she fought back the tears.

"Here." Jenessa handed her over to her.

Mikayla, like Jenessa, had nothing but love for Lil Kay. Shade was elated how his life was right now.

"Shade," Mikayla whispered his name and nodded toward the bed.

When he looked down, his wife was fast asleep.

"I'm going to update Jarvis." She carefully handed Lil Kay to him.

He took his daughter over to the chair and sat down. Mikayla came over, kneeling by him.

"Thank you for being the best big brother. I love you." She kissed his cheek and left before he said anything.

He knew she wasn't one to express herself well but understood how much he meant to her.

In the quietness, he studied his stunning daughter's face. She did mirror her mother, and he loved it. Her sleepy pouted lips were perfect. Her chunky cheeks were pinchable.

"Lil Kay, I'm your dad," he whispered tenderly to his daughter.

The tired baby opened her eyes briefly before closing

them again.

"I'm going to love you, protect you, and give you everything." He vowed to her.

Glancing over at his sleeping wife, he never felt so complete. He dreamt of this moment many times in his life. At one time he truly didn't believe it would happen with his broken marriage. However, it was clear the marriage was completely fixed, and he was heading toward a happily ever after with his wife and daughter.

WHAT'S NEXT?

Be on the look out for New Hampshire Bears' next installment!

You'll see it in the Spring of 2020.

Thank you for the support!

ABOUT THE AUTHOR

USA Today Bestselling Author, Mary Smith, has been coming up with stories her whole life. She has written over forty romance stories involving hot sports stars, strong willed females and everything in between. When not busy writing or rooting for the Chicago Blackhawks you can find her with her nose stuck in her Kindle.

You can visit her website at:
 www.authormarysmith.blogspot.com
Follow her on:
Instagram: @maryms1980
Facebook: www.facebook.com/authormarysmith

Books By Author:

The Ice Series (Adult Sports Romance trilogy):
(no longer in print or ebook) Melting Away the Ice
(no longer in print or ebook) Breaking the Ice
(no longer in print or ebook) Shattering the Ice
(no longer in print or ebook) Thawing the Ice (A Novella)

A Hockey Tutor (New Adult Sports Romance)
Dart and Dash (New Adult Sports Romance)
Always Forever (New Adult Rocker Romance)
DREAM (Adult Romance Suspense)

The Matched Trilogy (Paranormal Romance Trilogy):
A Royal's Love
A Protector's Second Chance
A Controller's Destiny

New Hampshire Bears Series (Adult Sports Romance)
The Muse and the Fairy Tale
The Workaholic and the Realist
The Hero and the Fat Girl
The Arrangement
The Coach and the Secret
The Captain and the Broken Girl
The Backup and the Baby
The Player and the Tattoo Artist
The Goalie and the Best Friend's Sister
The Lush and the Angel
The Nice Guy and the Therapist
The Devoted Father and the Introvert
The Opposite Attraction
The Broken Marriage

Books with author Lindsay Paige:

A Penalty Kill Trilogy (New Adult Sports Romance):
Breakaway
Off the Ice
Game Over
Our First Christmas (A Novella)

Oh Captain, My Captain Series (Adult Sports Romance)

Looking for You
A Hockey Player's Proposal
Finding Carson Lee
Let's Be Crazy
Their New Beginning
You and Me, Forever
Tainted

The Ninth Inning Series (Adult Sports Romance)
Felix
Blake
Hector
Trent
Jordan
Colby
Roman
Spencer
Tanner

Books with Melody Heck Gatto

Lattes and Slapshots (Grizzlies Book 1)

Wanted: Boyfriend for Christmas

Printed in Great Britain
by Amazon

56791018R00140